The Forbidden Woman

THE
FORBIDDEN
WOMAN

(L'INTERDITE)

Malika Mokeddem

TRANSLATED BY

K. MELISSA MARCUS

University of Nebraska Press
Lincoln and London

Publication of this translation was
assisted by a grant from the French
Ministry of Culture
Originally published as *L'Interdite,*
© Editions Grasset & Fasquelle, 1993
Translation and preface
© 1998 by the University of
Nebraska Press
All rights reserved. Manufactured
in the United States of America.
Library of Congress Cataloging-in-
Publication Data
Mokeddem, Malika. [Interdite.
English] The forbidden woman =
L'interdite / Malika Mokeddem;
translated by K. Melissa
Marcus. p. cm.
– (European women writers series)
Includes bibliographical references
ISBN 0-8032-3193-8 (cloth: alk. paper).
ISBN 0-8032-8240-0 (pbk.: alk. paper)
I. Marcus, K. Melissa, 1956– .
II. Title. III. Series.
PQ3989.2.M5515813 1998
843 – dc21 97-22024 CIP

CONTENTS

PREFACE

In an interview in 1994 Malika Mokeddem stated, 'All my life I have waged a battle to be whom I want to be in the face of a society that wanted to crush women. I dedicated myself to my studies, to the battle for women's rights, but I was suffocating. I had to leave. That is my failure. I write to raise my voice from the Midi [the southern coast of France], a voice other than that put forth by the [Muslim] fanatics, and to rid myself of this feeling of failure. I am from both coasts, a woman flayed alive, but also an angry woman' (*L'Humanité*, 15 April 1994, 18; all translations are mine).

As its title suggests, *The Forbidden Woman* tells of the struggle of one woman, Sultana, and, through her, of the struggle of Algerian women. In her native country Sultana is forbidden to do many things: to experience love and express it, to lead the life of an independent and successful career woman, to act on her own volition, to speak freely, smoke in public, go to a bar. Her rebellion against the forbidden and the resulting clashes between her and those who do the forbidding, the Muslim fundamentalists, are at the core of Mokeddem's third novel.

Born in Kenadsa, Algeria, a small mining town on the edge of the desert, Mokeddem spent her childhood in a *ksar*, a traditional village built of earth. She was the oldest of thirteen children and the daughter of illiterate nomads who only recently had become sedentary. She grew up listening to the stories told by her Bedouin grandmother, Zohra.

Although raised in a tolerant version of Islam, Mokeddem's battles against the weight of tradition and custom nevertheless began early. She was the only girl in her family and village who attended high school in the neighboring town of Béchar. Once there, she was the only girl in a class of forty-five students. Again, it was her nomad grandmother, Zohra, who played a major role in Mokeddem's life by insisting that her parents put her in school. 'She said that a sedentary person, which is what we had become, is someone whom death has taken by the feet, and there were only words to bring back the nomadic memory,' explained Mokeddem (*Elle*, 4 September 1995, 34).

Home from boarding school, she spent her summers inside the house, sheltered from the ferocious heat of the Saharan desert. As her increased knowledge and learning separated her from her milieu, she distanced herself further by reading late into the night and then sleeping half the day. She escaped from her oppressive world and moved toward a multitude of different worlds by immersing herself in the literary classics of Sartre, de Beauvoir, Faulkner, and Dostoyevsky, among others. With wry amusement, Mokeddem quotes her mother: 'There was always a book between me and my daughter.' She experienced not a mere distancing from her origins but indeed the first of several states of exile, culminating in her definitive departure from Algeria.

Mokeddem also broke tradition by refusing an arranged marriage. When an elderly uncle arranged the visit of a potential suitor's mother, Mokeddem climbed out the window and hid for the day. 'I saw my mother, I saw the women closed up inside their houses and subjugated. I did not want to become one of them. I did not want to grow up. I dreamed of going into the desert to die, to be devoured by jackals. I became anorexic' (*France catholique*, 23 November 1991, 21).

Mokeddem finished her high-school studies and went to medical school in Oran. She then went to Montpellier, France, where she specialized in nephrology, the branch of medicine that deals with the kidneys. She remained in Montpellier and married a Frenchman. After working as a nephrologist for several years, she discovered the importance of serving the mostly North African immigrant community in Montpellier –

particularly the women – and opened an office of general medicine in a largely immigrant neighborhood. She then began dividing her time between her writing and her practice.

Her writing consumed more and more of her time, and her books have been widely reviewed and well received. She is the author of two previous novels: *Les Hommes qui marchent* (The men who walk; Paris: Editions Ramsay, 1990) and *Le Siècle des sauterelles* (The century of the locusts; Paris: Editions Ramsay, 1992). *Les Hommes qui marchent* has just been reedited, and the new edition will appear this year. For *L'Interdite* (*The Forbidden Woman*), Mokeddem received the Prix Fémina's honorable mention and the Prix Méditerranée-Jeunesse (the Mediterranean Youth Prize). It is the first of Mokeddem's four novels to appear in English. She also finished a fourth novel, *Des Rêves et des assassins* (Of dreams and assassins; Paris: Editions Grasset), in 1995. It is possible that *The Forbidden Woman* will be adapted for the screen.

Because of the success of her novels, Mokeddem now writes almost full time. Also, a death threat at work influenced her decision to close her general practitioner's office. She now works in a nephrology clinic outside Montpellier approximately two days a week. Recently, in spite of the possible dangers to her, Mokeddem traveled to Algeria for the first time in several years. She returned home safely, enchanted with her trip and her reestablishment of contact with the Algeria that she loves.

In *The Forbidden Woman* Mokeddem has deftly woven the complex social and political contexts of the last thirty years of Algerian history into a novel that is both her personal story and an expression of solidarity with her people – particularly with women, but also with men, as both are the victims of the current upheavals in Algeria. Her anger is the anger of many, for *The Forbidden Woman* is solidly anchored in current events.

After the Algerian war of independence from France (1954–62), socialism, Arabization, and secularism were to be among the guiding principles with which to rebuild Muslim Algeria. The result was a glaring contrast between an officially socialist regime that endorsed liberation movements around the globe and a society that lived according to the imperatives of the Muslim religion. The single ruling party, the Front de Libération Nationale (National Liberation Front; FLN), allowed the existing patriarchal and Arab-Muslim traditions to rule the private spheres of Algerian life.

During the war of independence, however, Algerian women had participated fully and in many ways: as revolutionaries, in the underground, as messengers and weapon carriers. The new socialist society to be formed after Algeria's victory promised women equal and full participation in Algerian society. But the influence of the Islamic fundamentalists over twenty years' time led to the writing of one of the most reactionary family codes in North Africa. This code, passed in 1984, institutionalized the unequal status of Algerian women in matters of personal autonomy, divorce, polygamy, and the right to work outside the home. It legally empowered men over women. Women's groups, among them former revolutionaries, rallied against the code's passage, but the vulnerability of women as a social group was clearly revealed. The family code succeeded in erasing historical changes that had permitted the fuller participation of women in Algerian society – a change that had occurred in spite of the repression of the entire populace under colonial rule. Algerian women were brutally disappointed as the promises and dreams resulting from national liberation did not come to fruition for them.

The members of the elite who were to restructure and rebuild Algeria's society, educational system, and government were almost exclusively francophone. The country lacked a sufficient number of qualified teachers of Arabic to implement the policy of Arabization. To remedy this problem, thousands of mostly Egyptian and Syrian teachers were hired to teach Arabic in the nation's schools. The boundaries between Arabization and Islamization blurred, and officially declared secularism waned as revolutionary and conservative Islam was imported into Algeria with the teachers. The mosques became one of the few places for free expression, because the FLN repressed free discussion elsewhere. As many of the promises made during the revolution and after liberation were not fulfilled, an increasingly angry and disillusioned populace turned to the Islamists as a vote of confidence against the FLN.

The failures of the FLN were many. Algeria suffered and continues to suffer from housing shortages, so much so that many young couples must postpone marriage because there are not enough lodgings, outside of their parents' homes, for them to live in. The country does not have a sufficient number of schools or qualified teachers. There is severe unemployment, inflation, and extremely high foreign debt. The black market flourishes. Approximately 44 percent of Algeria's population is less than fifteen years old, and 56 percent is less than twenty years old. A large underclass of the young, keenly aware of the lack of a hopeful future for themselves, has been created. A new word has emerged, *haittites* (in French, *hittistes*) from the Arabic term *al hait,* meaning 'the wall.' It designates 'those who hold up the walls,' that is, loiterers, the unemployed, who stand around for hours with nothing to do except joke, whistle at girls, and pass the time by smoking. These are the idle and alienated young men of Algeria. In their anger, they and their families are the ideal target for the propaganda of the Front Islamique du Salut (Islamic Salvation Front; FIS). The FIS has infiltrated schools, neighborhoods, universities, and mosques and has successfully offered social services that the government and FLN have too often failed to offer, despite the clear and dire needs of the populace.

In the fall of 1988 the general dissatisfaction of the populace culminated in bloody riots. These were the first of the upheavals that would result in several critical events. In the December 1991 legislative elections the FIS won a plurality of votes, 47.4 percent. In January 1992 the government annulled the elections so the Islamists would not take power. The result was a series of violent clashes between the military and police and various militant Islamic groups. A wave of terrorist attacks followed, and President Muhammad Boudiaf was assassinated. In 1993 the attacks and bloodshed continued, as did a wave of assassinations targeting Algeria's government officials, as well as its finest intellectuals, writers, journalists, and artists, all carried out by the FIS and other extremist groups.

Today Algeria is still in a state of virtual civil war as government forces continue to clash with an array of militant Islamic groups. An estimated fifty thousand civilians have died in the last several years, killed by Islamic fundamentalists or by the ruling military government. Some of the conflict has been carried to French soil, as the Groupe Islamique Armé (Armed Islamic Group; GIA), angry at the French government for supporting the current Algerian regime, carries out terrorist attacks, mostly in Paris. It is in this climate of fear, lack of trust, and terror that Mokeddem wrote *The Forbidden Woman*. From the French side of the Mediterranean, *The Forbidden Woman* is a plea against the violence.

Mokeddem's novel is a cry of pain in the face of the Algerian woman's plight in dealing with the Muslim fundamentalists who, in the name of the Koran, are attempting to take away all of her rights. Mokeddem explains,

> In Muslim societies the individual does not exist: he or she exists only as the member of a tribe or clan and does not have the right to take initiatives. When it is a girl who takes the initiative to say 'I,' to assert herself, to be free, it is even more dramatic. For who holds the power of tradition? Who transmits the heritage of the absolute power of men? It is the women themselves. So when a girl reaches school and begins to challenge this tradition that crushes everyone, the traditional family completely loses its structure, becomes panicked. This is not the only origin of the fundamentalism surging forth here and there, but I believe that Muslim men are very worried. The rural exodus, immigration, unemployment, bad housing conditions, isolation, all weaken traditional family structures and break apart the tribe. The rebellion of a girl against her parents is considered to be a betrayal, and the reactions are violent. And if the girl has no support outside the tribe, true dramas can take place. (*Le Point*, 28 August 1993, 58)

Mokeddem's liberation came through school, education, and the world of ideas. Indeed, she claims that her 'only real community is the community of ideas' and that it is impossible for her, and for the novel's heroine, Sultana, either to return to Algeria or to fit in and adapt to France. At the heart of *The Forbidden Woman* is *métissage*, a French word and concept that so aptly describes the blending of cultures, languages, psychologies, and perceptions that results when people from different countries and backgrounds live together. Mokeddem presents us with the possibility of a harmonious and peaceful *métissage* for France and Algeria and, by implication, for other parts of the world. (On *métissage*, see Françoise Lionnet, *Autobiographical Voices: Race, Gender, Self-Portraiture*, Ithaca NY: Cornell University Press, 1989).

The hopes for Algeria are embodied in the appealing children of *The Forbidden Woman:* Dalila, who strives to reconcile society's contradictions, and Alilou, a quiet yet visionary and poetic child. Hope is also expressed by the solidarity of the women of the village, who, like their real-life counterparts, band together and rebel.

Mokeddem does not have a feeling for dry narrative. *The Forbidden Woman* has a sometimes breathless rhythm and indeed was written in urgency – in a mere ten months. If one prefers calm narration and is averse to a plethora of descriptive adjectives and seemingly incongruous metaphors, then one might consider Mokeddem's style excessive. Yet one cannot easily put down *The Forbidden Woman*. To ask of Mokeddem to 'polish' her verbose and lyrical writing would undoubtedly be an error. For she needs this intense prose to treat a subject about which she feels such passion, a subject so close to her own personal experiences. She needs the verbal excess to speak of the wounds of the Algerian woman who is trying to confront the bitter sorrows of Algeria. Her prose, a mix of dream and realism, has a vivid and cutting tone. She is patient and tenacious, and the force of her convictions shows through.

I would like to express my thanks to several people. I am very grateful to Maguy Albet for having introduced me personally to Malika Mokeddem; to Marie-Hélène d'Ovidio of Editions Grasset for her help, interest, and kindness; and to my dear friend, colleague, and fellow translator Marilya Veteto-Conrad and my mother, Arlen Bishop, for their repeated and careful proofreading of my work. Finally, I would like to warmly thank the author herself, Malika Mokeddem, for her hospitality in France, her help in answering my many questions, and above all her exceedingly courageous literary, political, and personal stance.

K. MELISSA MARCUS

The Forbidden Woman

To Tajar Djaout,
forbidden to live
because of his writings.

To the group Aïcha,
my Algerian women friends
who refuse to be forbidden.

In the vast colony of our being there are many different kinds of people, all thinking and feeling differently . . . And, like a diverse but compact multitude, this whole world of mine, composed as it is of different people, projects but a single shadow, that of this calm figure who writes . . .

– Fernando Pessoa, *The Book of Disquiet,* trans. Margaret Jull Costa

1

SULTANA

I was born on the ksar's only dead-end street.[1] A nameless dead end. This is my first thought in light of the immensity of what I will have to face. It envelops my turmoil with a cascade of silent laughter.

I would never have believed it possible to return to this place. And yet I've never really left it. All I have done is incorporate the desert and the inconsolable into my displaced body. They have split me in two.

From the top of the passenger steps, I look at Tammar's small airport. The building has been enlarged. The runways too. Tammar . . . in the whirlwinds of light, the years topple over and pile up to present time. It makes my heart sink. My oasis is a few kilometers from here. A ksar made of earth, a labyrinthine heart, bordered by dunes, fringed by palm trees. I see myself again as an adolescent girl leaving the region for Oran's boarding school. I remember the painful circumstances of that departure. As flight becomes rupture, as absence becomes exile, time itself shatters. What remains? A rosary of fears, the inevitable baggage of exodus. But when distance unites with time, you learn to conquer the worst fears. They tame us. So that we and our fears live together in the same skin, without being too torn. At certain moments, you can even jettison the inner conflict. Not just anywhere. In the most burning moment of guilt. When regret is most hidden. A privileged place of exile.

---

1. *Ksar:* traditional village built of earth (plural: *ksour*).

Blinking her eyes in the painful glare, the stewardess, with a smile, invites me to go down the few steps in front of me. I'm holding up the passengers.

Why this sudden desire to reestablish contact? Is it because I was sick of the world? A nausea resurfacing from things forgotten, through disenchantment with somewhere else and other places, in the harsh light of lucidity? I still found myself undone by everything. Once again, my detachment had erased my features, pinned a forced smile to my mouth, banished my eyes to the nether regions of meditation.

Or is it because Yacine's letter had been mailed from Aïn Nekhla, my native village?

No doubt a combination of all that.

It was on a very windy day. The violent north wind thrust the beginning of autumn's harsher weather into the warmth of a Montpellier caught off guard. It was also a day when nostalgia blew hard. Nestled in its howls, I listened to the north wind, I heard in myself the sand wind. And suddenly the need to hear Yacine, to be with him in that house, started to stir in me behind my censoring bars. Something still not subdued burst brutally forth from my prolonged lethargy. My thoughts, outward bound, suppressed my nausea, rekindled my homesickness. North wind outside, sand wind inside, my resistance dropped. Telephone, search, ringing, and this unknown voice:

'Who is this, please, Madam?'

'Sultana Medjahed, a friend of Yacine's. Is he there?'

'A very close friend?'

'Uhh . . . yes, why?'

'Madam, where are you calling from, please?'

'I'm in France. Why all these questions? Isn't Yacine there?'

'Madam, I regret to inform you that he died last night.'

'Died? Last night?'

'Yes, Madam, may Allah rest his soul. We discovered him in his bed. He looked like he was just sleeping. He, the athlete, in the best of health! Yesterday afternoon he played soccer with the village kids for a long time.

[4]

I'm the nurse who works with him. We're waiting for the doctors from Tammar, the next town.'

'Died last night.' My nausea had started to boil, to cook me. To calm it, I rocked myself in the blowing of the north wind and the sand wind mixed inside me. I lied to myself: This is only a nightmare, a black ram who has broken into the white field of my indifference. These are just lies or hallucinations, born of the meeting of two demented winds. These are nothing but reminiscence, the past lashing out against the desert of the present. Tomorrow nothing will remain of them. Tomorrow the sand wind will have buried the fears of childhood and adolescence. Tomorrow the north wind will have swept my Midi. Tomorrow my indifference will have once again filled in its gaps.

Suitcase in hand, I go toward a taxi.

'Can you take me to Aïn Nekhla please?'

'Whose daughter are you?' inquires the driver in a curt tone of voice, as he puts my suitcase into the trunk, amid the heap of tools and grease-stained rags.

'No one's.'

I get into the car and loudly slam the door to discourage the interrogation that I sense coming. He pushes back his chechia,[1] stares at me, scratches his forehead, spits on the ground, and finally consents to take his place behind the steering wheel. He starts up the engine, glancing at me frequently in the rearview mirror. Little burning glances, hungry glances that size me up as if I were a puzzle all in pieces that he didn't know how to begin.

'So, whose place are you going to in Aïn Nekhla?'

'No one's.'

'There's no hotel in Aïn Nekhla. How can you go to no one's place? Here, even a man can't go to "no one's place"! "No one" doesn't exist here!'

---

1. *Chechia:* a small, close-fitting, circular-shaped hat worn by men.

I have forgotten nothing. Neither this biting curiosity nor this meddling that asserts its rights over all.

When the inquisition is posed as civility, these questions are like a summons, and remaining silent is the admission of dishonor. The man stares at me in the rearview mirror and yells, ' "No one" doesn't exist! And there's no hotel!'

I have forgotten none of my past terror either. Under its influence, I closed my eyes to everything, banishing even those who showed me compassion. Only two women had been able to approach me and conquer me: an elderly neighbor and Emna, a Jewish woman from the mellah.[1] Mine was an isolation armored with silence.

This harassment makes me tense. I can no longer see the desert. I bring my eyes back to the man. Now I think I recognize him. One of the anonymous grimacing faces from the horde that used to persecute me. One of the faces of hatred. In that moment I withdraw. A moment from which I exclude him. I carefully envelop myself in my dissident and different Sultanas.

One is nothing but emotions, exaggerated sensuality. Her voluptuousness is painful, and bursts of sobs split her laughter. A tragedienne having so worn out her sorrow that it tears at the first assaults of desire. Unsated desire. Impotent longing. If I let her run free she would annihilate me. For now, she devotes herself to her favorite pastime: ambiguity. She swings the pendulum between pain and pleasure.

The other Sultana is sheer will. Demoniacal will. A curious mix of insanity and reason, with an outer layer of contempt and the sword of provocation permanently raised. A fury that exploits all, cunningly or ostentatiously, starting with the weaknesses of the other. Sometimes she delights me, only then to terrify me all the more. Vigilant and rigid, she coldly scrutinizes the landscape and with her goad keeps me at a respectful distance.

A gaping inner rictus distorts my attention.

1. *Mellah:* the Jewish quarter.

Having arrived in Tammar, the cabbie stops his heap in front of a grocer's store. He gets out without a word. I look at the street in alarm. It's crawling with people even more than in my nightmares. It shamelessly inflicts its masculine plurality and its feminine apartheid. The street is pregnant with every frustration possible, is tormented by every type of insanity and dirtied by all of its misery. Its ugliness hardened by a sun whitened with rage, it exhibits its welts, its wrinkles, and splashes about in the sewers with all of its urchins.

Some of them immediately congregate around the taxi. 'Madam! Madam! Madam! Madam!'

Long French-sounding onomatopoetic tirades from which emerge, here and there, a few rare words identifiable in Algerian and French: 'I love you . . . fuck . . . dick,' accompanied by gestures that couldn't be any more suggestive.

I have not forgotten that the boys of my country had a sick and gangrenous childhood. I have not forgotten their clear voices that ring only with obscenities. I have not forgotten that from the youngest age, the opposite sex is already a ghost among their desires, a confusing menace. I have not forgotten their angelic eyes, when they simper and pour forth the worst insanities. I have not forgotten that they viciously beat dogs, that they hurl stones and insults at passing girls and women. I have not forgotten that they are aggressive because they have never learned what a caress is, be it only that of a look, because they have never learned to love. I have not forgotten. But memory never shields one from anything.

The cabbie returns. He glances complicitously at the children before starting up the car. They grab onto it. Laughing, the man accelerates. I'm so afraid of an accident that I cry out. His face lit up by laughter, one of the children calls at me before letting go.

'Whore!'

I start. 'Whore!' More than the sorrowful spectacle of the street, more than the view of the desert, this word drives Algeria into me like a knife. Whore! How many times as an adolescent, still a virgin and already wounded, did I have this word vomited onto my innocence. Whore!

[7]

Treacherous word, for a long time I was able to write it only in capital letters, as if it were women's only destiny, their only divinity, the lot of rejected women.

With satisfied eyes, the man observes me in the rearview mirror. Our eyes are glued to each other, size each other up, confront each other. Mine defy him, tell him how vile he is. He's first to lower his eyes. I know he'll hold this offense against me. I try to concentrate on the countryside.

How many years did I travel this road twice a day? In the morning, to go to the secondary school. In the evening, to return to Aïn Nekhla. A twenty-kilometer stretch between my village and the town. Twenty kilometers of nothingness. I have forgotten none of this nothingness, either. The straightness of its tarred line. Its threatening sky that scorches the poetry of the sand. Its palm trees, poor exclamation points forever unquenched. The endless scrawl of its gravel deserts. The wind's sardonic fifths. Then the silence, the weight of eternity consumed. I even recognize those little dunes over there ... How silly of me! From their crescent shape, I've just realized they're shifting dunes formed by sandstorms. They move about at the mercy of the wind.

The hardly audible sound of a flute flows in me. It took me some time to notice it, to hear it. Its slitherings reach me, overtake me entirely. I don't know what it's saying.

The man drives so erratically that he elicits strange moaning sounds from the dying transmission. The shocks are so worn that I'm shaken about as if on a racing camel. When the wheels dig into the side of the road, a breath of sand sweeps through the taxi. The scent of this sand is the only welcoming embrace. It's perfumed with a plant that bubbles in cracked wheat soup.

'Has it rained lately?' I can't help suddenly asking.

'Yes, a little,' answers the man, his eyes wide open with surprise.

Three drops of rainfall suffice for a low-growing plant to conquer the dryness and immediately explode two days later into yellow flowers with a heady fragrance. I still don't know its French name.

Encouraged by my question, the man makes a fresh attempt: 'So, you, where do you come from?'

In Oran I had learned to scream. In Oran I always held myself in a position ready to fend off attacks. The anonymity of large foreign cities has taken the edge off of my anger, moderated my retorts. Exile has softened me. Exile is the territory of that which cannot be seized, of rebellious indifference, of the confiscated look.

I resolutely keep my face turned toward the car window. I let myself go in the bath of my familiar scents. I tune my ear to this tenuous flute hidden within me. The car swerves. My fear makes the man laugh jeeringly. With big turns of the wheel he does it again. Now the rearview mirror shows me the look of an insane man. It's only then that I notice the beard that blackens his face. I should have distrusted him.

'Nobody's daughter, who's going to nobody's house! Are you trying to fool me, or what? Since you refuse to speak, you might as well wear a veil!'

I feel a sense of relief at the first glimpse of Aïn Nekhla's houses in the distance.

'Can you drop me off at the hospital please?'

'Are you the tabib's sister? He's the only foreigner, a Kabyle!'[1]

I don't respond.

'But you, you don't look like a Kabyle. They say he's not married . . . Maybe you're his. . .?'

Is he going to dare say his whore? I challenge him with my look. Turning his eyes away from the rearview mirror, he mumbles, 'Why did this Kabyle come here? Even the Sahara's children go north or abroad when they become doctors or engineers. People don't come here unless they're in prison or because of some punishment! We in the south, we are a punishment, a prison cell or a garbage can for all of the Tell's nabobs.[2] They

---

1. *Tabib:* doctor (feminine: *tabiba*). Kabyle: a member of the Berber tribe from La Grande Kabylie, one of the mountain ranges of northern Algeria.

2. *Tell:* in North Africa, the name given to humid regions near the coast.

[9]

only send us the country's riffraff. The proof is that he's in with the RCD,[1] the tabib is! But he died two days ago. They're going to bury him this afternoon!'

Beyond the vengeful tone that triumphs in his voice, I hear 'They're going to bury him this afternoon.' That empties me of all indignation. I had counted on the fact that here the dead are buried the same day, the very afternoon of their death. I deliberately put off my trip for two days. But the doctor undoubtedly had the right to special treatment. Yacine awaited my arrival.

I think of this burial at the end of my travels. A yoke of fatigue crashes down on me. I lose the sound of the flute, wild and immodest in my innermost being just a short time ago, before I had recognized its melody.

'The city tabibs cut into him just like a sheep. I hope they put him in the refrigerator the day before yesterday; if not, he's not going to smell like a sheep but more like a hyena!'

With disgust he spits out the window and continues in his surly tone. 'They were looking for the cause of his death, so they said! Does God need to justify taking back what he's given?'

I ought to slap this vile person. The fire of this wish passes through me and goes out. I content myself with careful observation of the man. His jacket is dirty and torn. His eyes, crazed in the rearview mirror, have two drops of pus in their corners. A fly leaves one eye only to go to the other. His eyelids are red and swollen. Conjunctivitis, I think with detachment. How many children is he responsible for? Eight? Nine, ten? How many women has he worn out?

My staring irritates him. He turns away and continues his monologue. His voice is no longer any more than a distant annoyance. Everything seems so distant to me. The memories coming back to me have merely a bland, faded taste. I try to retrieve the lost serpentine sounds of the flute.

1. RCD: Rassemblement pour la Culture et la Démocratie (the Union for Culture and Democracy, a political party).

A moment goes by before I realize that the car has completely stopped. The volleys of words have gotten the better of my last vibrations of emotion. After fifteen years of absence and a haunting nostalgia, I've arrived in Aïn Nekhla without even noticing. Had this man not been here, I would have burst out laughing. I have the horrible feeling that my reunion with this region is going to lead straight to confrontation, and that a thousand nostalgic sentiments are still more tolerable than Algerian reality.

On my right, the hospital, just a little smaller, just a little more dilapidated than I had remembered. I pull myself out of the taxi. My suitcase has already been thrown to the ground. I had had the time to change a little money during the brief stopover at the Algiers airport. I give two bills to the man. He pockets them and sticks out his hand again.

'How much do I owe you?'

Now he's the one who remains silent. I take out a third bill. He seizes it and quickly leaves. Three hundred dinars? It's way too much. He undoubtedly thinks that my misconduct is worth at least some sort of ransom. If only this trip would cost me in money alone.

I'm right in front of the hospital. In some places, the low wall encircling it is almost entirely covered in sand. Men are crouching or standing along the whole length of the building. They stare at me. Here, present time seems to me nothing more than a decrepit past, my memories broken and dusty. It must be noon. I can't check the time. My watch is in my bag, and I feel hypnotized. My heart is in my head and bangs away.

I end up climbing the four steps to the landing. I push open the heavy wooden door. A shadowy light, like that in a mosque, fills the entryway. To the right I recognize the door of the consultation room, to the left those of the two waiting rooms. The scraping sound of a chair being pushed back reaches me from the back room, the treatment room. A man in a white smock appears. He comes toward me.

'Hello, madam.'

'I'm a friend of Yacine's.'

[11]

Taken aback, he looks at me for a moment.

'Did you call from France, the day before yesterday?'

I nod my head.

'Ah! That's fine, that's fine. I'm glad you're here, madam. I'm the nurse. In his death, I believe, Dr. Meziane will be glad to know that you're here. He had no family left.'

'No. They were all killed during the war.[1] He had only his mother. She died about two or three years ago.'

'The Tammar doctors were also his friends. They did an autopsy on him. He was in good health. They said "sudden death." That was quite a sudden death all right! The ambulance brought him back this morning. He's just had the last ablutions. He's being buried at three o'clock.'

His eyes fill with tears. He turns his back to me and says, 'Come!'

I leave my suitcase and follow him. At the very end of the hallway, next to the treatment room, he opens the door to the morgue. The enormous form of a body lies wrapped in a shroud. Another one, a child, lies on a board on the ground. The odor of cadavers is strong.

'If you want to see him one last time, I can uncover his face.'

'No!'

My panicked cry sounds out of place in the silence. I'm ashamed of it. The nurse looks at me. I move toward the table. I hold out my hands and grab the form by its feet. Two or three layers of starched cloth separate me from it. I feel like I'm touching cardboard. What have I come to look for? The certainty that I'll never see him again, never again? Suddenly, Yacine appears before me, the way he would meet me in the hallways of the Oran hospital when we were students. He's in black corduroy pants and a green shirt, the same dark green of his eyes. His smile digs a broad dimple into his chin. He opens his arms to greet me. I rush toward him. But the atmosphere cuts into my breath. The shroud's whiteness burns my eyes. I hate this white, a scar in the half light. I hate this silence where the unspeakable explodes. I hate this stench. I would like to be able to scream,

---

1. The Algerian war of independence from France, 1954–62.

[12]

scream. My breathing blocked, I can't manage a moan or a word. I leave the room.

The nurse is at my heels and grabs my suitcase.

'I'll drive you to my house. My wife will take care of you. It's better that you go there.'

'No. I'm staying here. I'll go to Yacine's after the burial.'

'They won't let you attend his funeral. You know that women aren't allowed at funerals.'

'We'll just see who's going to stop me!'

'The mayor belongs to the FIS.[1] He didn't like Dr. Meziane, but he'll come. He won't miss an occasion so favorable to his propaganda. They're a few guys all stirred up and doing their best to enroll a populace dozing in its misery and taboos.'

I can't think of anything to say. I turn the door handle of the examination room. Everything is like before, except perhaps, for the examining table. A long white smock hangs behind the desk.

'Okay, you can just wait there, but . . . have you eaten?'

'I'm not hungry.'

'I'll make some coffee, at least.'

Visibly disappointed, he disappears without waiting for my answer. I close the door. My eyes go around the room. The window with its eternal mosquito net projects the light here and there, on the partly rusted X-ray machine, on the lead apron whose big tear is mended with adhesive tape, on the little glass-windowed metal cabinet where the few small bottles seem orphaned, on the cart emptied of its instruments, on the old tile flooring. The hanger. The long smock. Over there, the body under the shroud. An abandoned shroud here, in a heap of whiteness. To one side of the desk, an old armchair, to the other, three fake leather chairs. At the end of the room, the examining table. I'm going to sit down in the armchair. I back it up to the wall. The smock brushes lightly against my back,

---

1. FIS: Le Front Islamique du Salut (the Islamic Front of Salvation), a radical Islamic party and movement. See the preface.

[13]

my shoulders, my neck, my head. I caress it, sniff it, bury my face in it. Is this Yacine's odor? I no longer know what his odor was like. The cadaver's odor is still blocking my nose.

The hospital door opens abruptly. I immediately hear the nurse exclaim, 'Si Salah!'

Salah Akli? Yacine's best friend?

In the entrance hall, the two men exchange a few words. Suppressed sobs strangle their voices. I hear them going toward the morgue. A moment later they're back, and they come into the consultation room. I had seen Salah on only a few rare occasions. He was studying medicine in Algiers at the time, and I had always invented a thousand pretexts so as to avoid his meetings with Yacine. Was it out of jealousy? Was it out of fear? His jaundiced gaze is unforgettable.

'Madam. . . ?' the nurse asks me.

'Sultana Medjahed. Salah Akli and I know each other.'

'Oh, very good, very good.'

Quite obviously reluctant, Salah shakes my hand, looking at me with his mysterious cat's stare, while the nurse slips out.

'You never bothered to visit him or even answer his letters. But you arrive in time for his burial! He carried you in him like a deep abscess. Maybe that's what killed him! I've always wondered what he found in you that another less complicated woman couldn't have offered him,' he mutters between his teeth.

His words suffocate me. I'm looking for a stinging retort when Khaled returns carrying the coffee. For the moment, I rein in my anger. The man hands us the cups. The three of us drink in silence.

'Did you buy the sheep, Khaled?' Salah asks.

'Yes, I sacrificed it yesterday. This evening I'll take some plates of couscous to the mosque. I asked the talebs to be there.'[1]

'Thank you. Let me know what I owe you.'

'There's already a crowd in front of the hospital.'

---

1. *Taleb:* teacher at the Koranic school.

[14]

'Yes, there are a lot of people outside,' answers Salah.

'Now we're just waiting for the city doctors and the officials from here.'

Khaled hasn't finished his sentence when we hear a commotion in the hallway.

'Here they are!'

The office door opens on a group of men who block the entryway. Some of them move toward the end of the hallway. A droning sound of muffled voices, a dull sound of trampling feet, and Khaled reappears at the doorstep.

'Let's go!'

Salah and I leave. Outside, a male crowd. A broad age span, but predominantly young. The stretcher, carried by four men, bursts through the wide open door. They take their places at the head of the funeral procession, lining up with the men first, and a large number of adolescent males and children crowding in behind.

'La illaha ill'Allah, Muhammad rassoul, Allah!'[1]

The oneness of Allah, chanted, is the signal to leave. The procession gets underway. Khaled, Salah, and I follow. In the lead group, a man turns around several times. The fire in his eyes is unequivocal. He ends up retracing his steps and coming toward me.

'It's the mayor,' Khaled whispers to me.

'Madam, you can't come! It's forbidden!'

Salah takes me by the arm. 'Forbidden? Forbidden by whom?'

'She can't come! Allah doesn't want her to!'

'Well it so happens that Allah told her she could! She came from very far away for this!'

'You are profaning the name of God!'

'No more than you are!'

And pulling me by the arm, Salah drags me along with him. The man remains silent. We go past him. Regaining control of himself, he immedi-

---

1. *La illaha ill'Allah, Muhammad rassoul, Allah:* There is no God but God. Muhammad is his prophet.

ately follows on our heels screaming the chahada like a vengeful curse, a hurried appeal to the divine anger that we're risking.[1]

'Who is that?'

'Bakkar, the head of the FIS.'

'Bakkar!'

'Do you know him?' asks the nurse.

I don't answer. I've just discovered other eyes that won't release me, those of the man in the taxi.

'And he, who is he?'

'Ali Marbah, Bakkar's follower, a shady trabendist.'[2]

I am blazing with anger. I tug myself free from Salah's grasp.

'Pardon me,' he says.

I put my hands in my pockets. My fists squeeze, wrinkle the cloth. I lengthen my stride until I reach the head of the funeral procession. At the head of the crowd, I walk toward the cemetery. Little showers of stones punctuate our passage. I'd forgotten this local custom of repudiating death, of signifying to the corpse that it mustn't envy any of the living, nor try to drag anyone along with it.

As I'm pushed along by the unfolding waves of prayers, I discover an enormous village, a tumorlike growth in the side of the ksar. I'm not familiar with these streets that offer themselves, naked, to the sun's sadistic heat. My eyes miss the ksar. The winding shape of its alleys used to capture dreams, used to shelter flight and melancholy feelings. Intertwined shadows and light created by balconies and walkways built closely together, and the ocher colors of the earthen walls, wove a feeling of harmony. Now these constructions, in ruins even before they've been finished, display their cracks, their chaos, and their garbage, symbols of the ugliness and stupidity of the times. And the wisdom and patience of the elders have disappeared under the crammed-in youth, in the fire of its despair. I don't recognize a single face. But have I ever looked at normal

---

1. *Chahada:* the oneness of God. One of the five pillars of Islam.
2. *Trabendist:* one who engages in *trabendo:* smuggling, black market activities.

people? It was only the different faces of tyranny that forced me to be blind.

I turn toward the remains bouncing on the stretcher to the rhythm of the men's steps, to the rhythm of their voices chopping into God's oneness. It seems to me but one of the scenes from the tragic drama of the streets. Yacine is not here. He continued my flight. Our love has never been anything but that: flight. What did I come here to find? I have the unpleasant sensation of having yielded to something whose origin was indecency, to a sort of desire for voyeurism. I should never have revisited these places from my past. The little girl that I was is still there among the shadows of other children who had a similar fate. Suffering has preyed upon them ruthlessly, has grown up in their stead while disfiguring this place.

They bury him hastily. Hastily, they say a last prayer. I turn away from them and go back toward the hospital. For the first time since my arrival, I see the sky. It flows into me, completely fills me. A blue serenity checks the flow of my anguish. My step becomes firmer. Salah joins me again, and we walk side by side.

'It's been ten years since you've seen Yacine, right?'

'Yes, and more than fifteen years since I've been back to Aïn Nekhla.'

'Ten years! Sometimes the Mediterranean is impassable.'

'The abyss is in ourselves . . . I recognize nothing here.'

'You lived in the ksar?'

'Yes. It's where I was born.'

'The ksar has been completely deserted.'

'Yes, I had heard that. That had strengthened my desire not to return.'

'Some people in love with the Saouran ksour alerted UNESCO.¹ I don't know if they'll get anything out of it.'

I can't begin to imagine the ksar's being dead. I don't know if I'll have the courage to go there. Silently we continue on our way. Again I hear the flute. I feel it more than I hear it. It seems to be from another time, in my still inaccessible self.

1. *Saoura* refers to a wadi in the Algerian Sahara lined with palm groves. A wadi is a valley, ravine, or watercourse that is dry except during the rainy season. Saoura is also the name of one of the Algerian departments.

[17]

2

VINCENT

Something bombards my sleep. I open my eyes. I turn over onto my back and, dazed, feel the weight of the silence. But just as quickly the muezzin's call explodes again and torpedoes my lethargy. My consciousness flows. A consciousness aware only of existing, with no hold on it, weightless, as if beyond memory. Then, little by little, the scene imprints itself on me, surrounds me and delivers me to present time.

'Oh, the hell with it! For three nights the muezzin have been persecuting me!'

Oran, Aïn Sefra, Tammar, already three Algerian nights of this prayer that seems to be always chanted by the same voice.

The window is wide open. It cuts out a navy blue rectangle with a fluorescent glow of indigo. The juicy dawn drips into the room's darkness. Night draws itself in and secretly clears away its black flakes.

It's impossible for me to escape this voice any longer. It rises up menacingly from another epoch. It suffocates me. The day's prayers are nothing more than a high point among the exotic local sounds. Then why does this prayer disturb me so much? Is it because of this hybrid moment torn apart between two conflicting desires? Is it because it catches my vulnerability in a state of total abandonment? In it I hear something morbid, the moaning of the night, its throat, like that of an Aïd sheep, slit by some cosmic power.[1] And dawn in its birth is no more to me than this agony. I must know what this prayer says. I am persuaded that only then will I escape from this stranglehold.

'Poor Vincent, next time you'd do better to choose a hotel far away from any mosques, at least when possible. That would certainly be better for you!'

Damn! I think I'm ready to brave the desert, yet the sound of an unusual voice is enough to give me the blues. My attempt at humor rings hollow. I am more and more tense. I leap up and go to the window. On my left, the village, then the ksar, both slumbering. Across the way, the first upended strip of the western erg and the palm grove.[2] In the chiaroscuro of early dawn the palms stand erect and the dunes lie in waves. Curves and straight lines linger above the remains of the night. The dreamy half light of this scene banishes my apprehension. For a moment I lose myself in its contemplation. Then I return to my bed and stretch out on it.

Finally the muezzin shuts up. Shortly afterward a murmur tells me that the faithful are leaving the mosque. I try unsuccessfully to fall asleep again, even though in the last three days I've become so tired and had such insomnia. Shall I take a walk? I'm wholly unused to the morning hours. I'm a night person. Aren't these fevers and this anxiety the first signs of my body's rejecting the transplanted organ? My hand immediately moves to the scar on my right side. My index finger trembling, I trace the scar's slightest lines up and down, written with the providential scalpel, which, one day, placed a foreign kidney among my entrails. Foreign?

The doctors in Paris couldn't stop rejoicing. 'Mr. Chauvet, your tissue matches exactly that of the donor's kidney! What extraordinary luck!'

1. *Aïd al fitr:* the celebration marking the end of the Ramadan fast. *Aïd al ad'ha:* the sacrificial feast, for which a sheep is slaughtered.

2. *Erg:* a region of the Saharan desert covered with dunes.

First of all, they should have said 'female donor.' And anyway, 'she' didn't donate anything. Chance laid a diabolical trap for her, an ambush on her path: an auto accident, a lengthy coma, a dead future. She became no more than a numbered butcher's kidney for the profit of France Transplant. Happenstance is a cruel angel. I was a potential and preferential recipient on its checkerboard.

I had already been waiting several months for this transplant. But I'd never thought of the 'donor,' and anyhow, who among us on the transplant waiting list concerns himself with the origin of the hoped-for organ? How can you think, or even imagine, that being part of this list automatically gives you the right to a kidney still walking around, if I may put it this way, still in the warmth of the original abdomen, still in the blood of its first body? Yet we all know that these kidneys don't grow in greenhouse-laboratories. But damn it all! Let's not be fainthearted. All the killjoy questions that might disturb expectations go right through the trapdoor of the unconscious. I wasn't rushing the other person to his death. The increase in my desire for an organ didn't depend on anyone. Not on anyone – that's that. This kidney that I so yearned for belonged to no one, had no origin. It was born from the magic wand of a fairy named France Transplant, the day that she finally deigned to interest herself in one hoping and despairing case. So I was impatient with anticipation, feeling no guilt.

But the Other was there at the first quivering signs of consciousness, as I awoke from surgery. There, sewn to my body by pain, at the wound in my skin.

'Who is it?' I asked the intern bending over me.

'It's me. Don't worry Mr. Chauvet, everything is fine.'

'No, the kidney, who is it?'

'I'm not allowed to tell you. Stay calm, Mr. Chauvet, you're on an IV. Your kidney is pissing just fine.'

'Yes, yes, tell me,' I begged in my half-conscious state.

'It's the kidney of a twenty-seven-year-old Algerian woman. I won't tell you any more.'

A woman. A young woman. An Algerian woman. In shock, I think I once again took refuge in the anesthesia for a little longer. I didn't want to know anymore.

For several days I was torn apart by conflicted feelings. I couldn't be happy. My friends called it 'sentimentalism.' I stayed quiet. I hid my turmoil.

Little by little, however, my deliverance from the hellish artificial kidney machine, from the difficulty of such a dehumanized regimen, from the meager days whose link was that they were either with or without dialysis, covered up my troubled feelings. My newfound freedom, my physical deterioration now arrested, the resumption of projects and hope, helped me find a routine. I accepted the kidney. Or is it maybe the kidney that ended up integrating me into it and digesting, filtering, and pissing out all my tormented feelings? Without rejecting the organ, without failure. A mutual assimilation and truce. 'Excellent tolerance of the transplant. It was your own kidney we transplanted!' reveled the doctors. But this tolerance couldn't keep me from thinking that with this organ, surgery had implanted in me two seeds of strangeness, of difference: the other sex and another 'race.' And the feeling of this double *métissage* of my flesh became deeply rooted in my thoughts and pushed me uncontrollably toward women and toward this other culture, which until then I had haughtily disregarded. My frequent visits to Belleville and Barbès cured me of two other defects: resignation and loneliness.[1] Being resigned to being alone.

Daring to press harder, I feel around the arch-shaped transplant scar with my fingertips. It's there, tiny, firm, and oblong, and there's no sign of rejection. It hasn't taken advantage of my short sleep to rebel. My pulse is calm. I'm neither clammy nor hot. This brief examination, my first reflex in the morning, allows me to relax completely. Then, as always upon awakening, I catch myself caressing my transplant with a nostalgia of soul

---

1. Belleville, Barbès: Parisian neighborhoods where the population is largely North African.

and fingertips, for this forever unknown body, this foreign woman with the same identity, my female Algerian twin. When I can't see myself lying in the dark, I often open my arms to welcome her, to close them around her absence. I embrace her absence, I squeeze the emptiness of her presence. A kidney, almost nothing, a flaw, a simple twist of fate, unites us beyond life and death. We are a man and a woman, a Frenchman and an Algerian woman, Siamese twins, survival and death.

Why have I been so nervous ever since I've been in her native country? Is it because of the colossal boredom welling up out of the overpopulated housing projects? Is it because of the almost total absence of women in the street, especially at night? An absence that reinforces hers. That excludes her even more from this country. That precludes my immersion in this femininity of which I carry a fragment? Here, at certain moments, it's as if I were no more than a shred of her left living after her death. A disastrous feeling.

I felt peaceful during my long trip by sailboat down the length of the Spanish coast. By day I navigated. Rocked by the waves, I made sure that I did nothing that kept me from tasting any given moment. A gourmet's savoring. I reread books that I loved. I was amazed always to uncover, in the turn of a phrase, behind the reef of some too-significant word, a subtle and hidden meaning. I dreamed. I dreamed of Her, my absent woman in me, my Harlequin double, my rainbow identity. Sometimes we lived together for the duration of some dream. What exactly did we experience? A hazy sweetness, children's games inaccessible to reality's corruption. Upon awakening I tried to give her a face and a body again. But she slipped away. She resisted me like the deeper meanings hidden under the superficial meanings of a word. She left me only the outline of her kidney, the feeling of her absence. I caressed her through this kidney. I tamed her in all the meanings of nothingness. And to sail toward Algeria to the rhythm of the light autumn winds, to the rhythm of my blood traveling through her flesh, made me happy. I was going to read who she was, discover her, construct her through the voices, gestures, and behavior of thousands, millions of Algerian women. This feeling of well-being was

[22]

certainly linked to the progressive increase in temperature as I headed south. In the space of a few days, between Cadaques and Alicante, I experienced the change of the seasons. In the flow of time, I was in an imprecise state of suspense. A child in a cradle brought by a thread of water to the original womb of Africa.

Finally the day has taken over. My eyes inspect the room. I like to find myself in bare hotel rooms. Rooms without memory, available for many liberties, rooms that break all habits. I like waking up with daily things absent. I've always thought the cult of objects was linked to infantilism or fetishism. You've never had a soul, you inanimate objects! You're just stillbirths. Our dead hopes, like the graveyard's recumbent statues, tombstones of our moments, our mummified illusions. In my room in Paris there are nothing but books around my bed, just ink souls enclosed in their paper dreams.

I get up and go to the window. The erg is fixed in its rusty copper color. At the top of the first dune I distinguish a small silhouette. So early in the morning! Is it a boy or a girl? I slip on a shirt and jeans and leave my room. The hotel is deserted. The front door isn't locked. Outside the air is mild and a crystalline silence reigns over the palm grove. I hastily climb up the dune. When I'm halfway to the top, the small silhouette gets up, descends two steps quickly in my direction, and comes to a halt. It's a little girl. I stop too. I need to catch my breath. As I make my way up the dune, I have the impression that the sand is gradually coursing upward in me like mercury in a thermometer. I make an effort not to let myself sink. My legs, heavy with sand, no longer carry me except by sheer will. The girl backs up slowly, regaining her perch at the top. She's very brown, but I can't yet distinguish her features. I continue climbing toward her.

'Hello,' I say when I finally reach the summit.

She smiles at me. She's no more than nine or ten years old. She has dark, long eyes that look at me obliquely. Curly hair surrounds her delicate little face. I let myself drop onto the dune a few steps from her, my body covered with and flowing into the sand.

[23]

'You, are you French?'

'Yes.'

'Why didn't Yacine come with you?' she worries with a sound of disappointment in her voice.

'Who's Yacine?'

'Aren't you his friend? When I saw you I thought it was him. You have yellow hair like him.'

'No. I don't know him.'

'There's always his friends who come and see him from the Tell and even LaFrance, sometimes.'

'I don't know him,' I repeat stupidly, sorry about such an inability to answer.

'He was supposed to come the morning before yesterday. But he didn't come. I came here to wait for him, even in the evening and even yesterday. He didn't come. He was supposed to bring me the book from an Algerian man from LaFrance, a migrant. He didn't come. He said that it's a book for all children, from LaFrance and from here. He didn't come.'

Her lower lip trembles slightly and her distress grows a little more each time she says, 'He didn't come.'

'You know, boys sometimes forget their promises . . .'

'He's not a boy! He's a doctor! He never forgets, he doesn't! He never lies!'

She is yelling. Instead of consoling her, I've offended her. She lets me know by confronting me with a glum expression.

'A doctor who takes care of sick people?'

She shrugs her shoulders. Out of spite or because of the absurdity of my question?

'Then his car must be broken down,' she decrees, and then quickly adds: 'because he can't be sick, he can't be. He's a doctor.'

'Listen, I need to see a doctor anyway. If you tell me where his office is, I'll go see him. That way I'll be able to tell you what happened.'

'But he's not here! He's a doctor at the Aïn Nekhla Hospital, the next village over.'

[24]

'Well, then I'll go to Aïn Nekhla.'

'Really, you'll go to Aïn Nekhla?' she inquires, doubtful.

'Yes, I promise you.'

That seems to comfort her.

'And he comes to see you in the morning from so far away?'

'He makes pictures, even with paint. Sometimes he sleeps at the hotel and he comes to draw the palm trees, the dunes, and the sun when it's coming up. Sometimes he also comes when it's going down. Once he drew me for a long time. He wants to give me the picture. I'd like it a lot. But I'm afraid.'

'Afraid of what? Afraid of the picture?'

'Noooo!' She laughs at my ignorance before continuing. 'At home they'll yell. They'll hit me. They won't let me go out anymore. They'll cut me off from school.'

'Then you're right to be scared. They mustn't see this painting.'

'Yacine also says "painting."'

'This portrait, do you like it?'

'Yes. But it's not like a picture. It's as if I were seeing myself in a dream . . . he draws every morning, Yacine does. Sometimes he does nothing but mix colors, but it's still pretty. When the sun is up he says, "Nothing left to do but go to work!" Then he goes and is a doctor in Aïn Nekhla. But this time he was supposed to come and he didn't . . .'

She lowers her eyes and doesn't finish her sentence. Embarrassed, she digs into the sand with her forefinger. Then, as if just reminded of something, she turns around and scrutinizes the dunes. I don't see anything in that direction; rust-colored dunes stretching to infinity in the soft morning light.

'She left because of you!' she declares, her finger pointed toward the width of the dunes.

'Whom did I make leave? There aren't any footprints.'

'She doesn't make any footprints when she walks, she doesn't!'

'Who is she?'

She remains silent.

'Whom did I make leave?'

She smiles mysteriously, but she doesn't answer. I don't insist for fear of irritating her again.

'Do you go to school?'

She hesitates.

'Are you learning French at school?'

'Yes, for the last three years. But I've been learning it for four years, a lot at home so I can read my sister's letters and write to her. The others never write to her.'

'Where's your sister?'

'In LaFrance.'

'Oh I see. . . ! And why are you the only one who writes to her?'

'Well, my dad, he doesn't know how to write, and anyway, he had a fight with her. He only knows how to send her curses. My brothers fought with her too, even those who don't have . . .'

She finishes her sentence by making a gesture all around her face with her hand.

'Even the ones who don't have a beard? Who aren't Islamists?

'Yes, three of them don't have a beard and aren't Islamists, but they still don't like her.'

'And why not? What did she do to them?'

'She doesn't like to obey and doesn't want to marry. They've found a lot of husbands. But she always says no. She's still studying; now she's studying in LaFrance. And afterward she doesn't want to come here anymore. She didn't come . . .'

She shows me her right hand with her fingers spread apart. Her lower lip begins to tremble again.

'For five years? Five years is a long time, isn't it?'

'Yes, that's why I'm trying hard in French. When I leave school I go to Ouarda's, Rabah's wife. She's a schoolteacher at the secondary school.'

'The word is professor.'

'Yes, professor. I've rented myself out at her house. I watch her baby. Not for money – so she'll teach me. I study a lot on my own too, and I show her my homework when she has time. She's really nice. She says I'm making big progress. Very quickly. It's quiet in her house. Her husband always works far away. So I sleep at her house. Sometimes I even sleep there when he's home. I like to sleep over there. We talk about my sister, Samia. I write to her. And then Ouarda makes me read. It's nice!'

Her expression, happy again, leaves no doubt about her complicity with this teacher.

'You say it's quiet in her house. Is there a lot of noise at your house?'

'Yes, I have too many brothers. They make too much noise. They fight all the time. They fight with me, and they even fight with my mother. They're always saying to me, "You're not going out! Work with your mother! Bring me something to drink! Give me my shoes! Iron my pants! Lower your eyes when I talk to you!" and on and on and you multiply it by seven. They yell and do nothing but give me orders. Sometimes they hit me. My mother, she's happy when I'm with Ouarda because I can read and do schoolwork. But she also says, "Obey your brothers. If you don't, you're not my daughter." '

'Samia is your only sister, isn't she?'

She agrees and her face clouds over.

'Are you sure that the others don't miss Samia?'

'My mother does. Sometimes my mother cries and hides her tears. If my father sees her crying he yells and says he doesn't want anyone to talk to him about Samia anymore, never, and that if she comes back he'll kill her. The mailman always leaves me her letters at Ouarda's house. But when I was alone with my dad in the street, three times he said to me like this: "Is your sister okay?" I was afraid of him. I didn't want to say anything to him. But his eyes didn't look mean. His eyes were sad. So I said yes, only with my head, that way he couldn't blame me for anything. Sometimes my dad does like this.' She heaves a long sigh. 'And he says, "Ya Allah!" Then I say to myself: he's thinking of Samia and he doesn't want to admit it. When my mama talks about her, my brothers say that Samia is a whore. It's not true! Samia, she just wants to study and walk in the street when she wants to and be left alone. My brothers only think about

[27]

her so they can insult her. Sometimes they say to me, "You'll never go to the 'versity! We won't let you do like Samia!" '

'The university?'

'Yes, the university.'

'They're afraid you'll follow the same path as your sister?'

'Yeah, the same path, because I work hard at school.'

'That's great!'

Her smile is fierce and radiant.

'But Ouarda always tells me, "Work hard and don't say anything to your father and brothers." She says I'll go away and study even after the university if I want to. My parents like her. They'll listen to her. Anyway, they'll be really old! That's what Ouarda says.'

'She's probably right.'

The sun has risen and is starting to heat things up. We stay quiet for a moment. Once again her eyes attentively scan the dunes.

'Who are you looking for?'

'Even when it's Yacine, she leaves.'

'Don't you want to tell me who walks without leaving footprints?'

She doesn't answer.

'Do your parents let you come here so early?'

'They don't know I'm here. I come here when I sleep at Ouarda's house. In the evening when they don't find me at home, they always think I'm at her house. My dad is always at the café playing dominoes. My mama, she works in the house. She doesn't go out.'

'And your brothers?'

'My brothers can't come and check for me at Ouarda's. They respect her. Two of my brothers work, three are haittites, and the two youngest ones are still in school.[1] But they're too lazy. Ouarda, she says if they continue like that, they'll be turned out from school.'

'You mean suspended?'

1. Haittites (French: *hittistes*): those who 'hold up the walls,' that is, loiterers, the unemployed, the rejected.

[28]

'Yes, sent home. When Ouarda says that to my dad, he hits them with his belt. He yells, "Do you wanna be like me? You wanna kill me?" But they keep doing the same thing.'

'And what's your mama think of all this?'

'My mom, she says like this, that it's "poverty that does it." She says that Independence is unfair. Sometimes she's so sad that she says that Allah, him too, he's unfair. When she says that in front of them, my Islamist brothers yell and fight with her. They say that she'll go to hell. I don't want her to, I don't. Do you think my mom will go to hell?'

'Oh, no! Hell doesn't exist.'

'You're from LaFrance. It's not the same. It's not the same hell . . . My mom, she always does this.' She illustrates her words with a shrug of her shoulders before continuing. 'And she says, "Hell is every day, it's now." She says that afterward, when she's dead, she'll finally have some peace.'

Suddenly she gets up. 'I have to go drink my coffee. Then I'm going to school.'

'Come and have breakfast with me at the hotel. Do you want to?'

'No, I can't. The people who work at the hotel, they'll tell my brothers. They'll hit me.'

'You think they'll tell them?'

She nods a vigorous yes and takes off running. Suddenly she stops and turns back toward me. Flooded by the sun, one foot planted in the sand, the other one drawing arabesque shapes with a graceful movement of her ankle, she's dark honey-colored and her hair gives off violet-colored rays. Her yellow dress floats around her like a butterfly wing.

'Do you think the Sahara is big?'

'Oh, yes, very big. It's even one of the biggest spaces not including the oceans.'

She stares at me perplexed before adding: 'In her letters, Samia says she always walks in the street. Do you have to walk to find space? Like nomads?'

'Maybe.'

Obviously, my answer leaves her unsatisfied. For a moment she remains undecided.

[29]

'Ouarda, she says that over there, too, Samia doesn't have her space because she's a foreigner and Samia's a foreigner everywhere. Ouarda says that lots of people are like that. Is it true?'

'Maybe.'

She looks at me angrily and explodes. 'Why do you always say "maybe"? You, you're big, you come from LaFrance. You know!'

'Well, you see, I know that the word "maybe" is often a bigger space than certainty is. I mean bigger than always knowing.'

Does she understand my answer? Does she adjust to it out of necessity? She turns toward the dunes, contemplative for a moment before continuing. 'Ouarda says that dreaming is also a space.'

'Yes, that's right! It's even the biggest of spaces.'

That entirely satisfies her. She takes off running. 'Wait! Wait!' I say, louder than I would have wanted to. In one leap she faces me.

'What's your name?'

'Dalila.'

'Dalila, that's very pretty.'

She laughs. 'And you?'

'My name is Vincent.'

'What's Vincent mean?'

'Nothing, it's the name of a saint, like a wise man.

'So you have to say "Sidi-Vincent"?'

'Sidi?'

'Yeah, for wise men, you say "Sidi." '

'But I'm neither a saint nor a wise man.'

She has a laugh like a nightingale's trill. She points her index finger at me. 'You promised to go see Yacine!'

'Yes, yes, I'll go tomorrow. Today I want to walk around here a bit. I just arrived last night.'

She starts running again. With a feeling of regret I watch her race down the dune. Having arrived at the bottom, she stops, turns around, motions to me with her hand, and starts running again.

I stay there, stretched out on the sand. The noise of the village reaches me now. The sun feels so good. The sky is immense, an intense periwinkle blue. Where do the people of Dalila's dreams live? I'll have to ask her.

It wouldn't be such a bad idea to go and consult this doctor. I have to check my blood pressure and my creatinine level every so often. I might as well go to this 'Doctor Yacine.' Last night, I'd located Aïn Nekhla on the map. It's very close by. This morning, do nothing, and then a walk.

Hunger overtakes me. I get up and go toward the hotel.

3

SULTANA

'Yacine had told me that you knew this house,' Salah called out to me, putting the key in the lock.

'Yes, I came here very often during my adolescence. I was sick and the doctor here at that time, Doctor Challes, had taken care of me a lot.'

Once the door is open, Salah moves aside to let me in. The smell of paint welcomes us. This house . . . in its grip, my memory panics between past and present. Time undergoes a contraction, a condensing. Yacine is here, in the past and in the present. His paintings have taken over the surroundings. I rediscover the aesthete in his ability to display and sanctify utilitarian objects. In a few movements, a few touches, he imbues them with unusualness and with the nobility of art.

During my entire trip I waited for this instant. I was waiting to be able to enter this place and close the door again behind me, to attempt to reconstruct a scattered past: a few small islands of happiness gnawed away by years of autism and aphasia and the cracks caused by absences and departures. Salah bothers me. He wanders aimlessly from one room to another. We hardly catch each other's eyes, even for only a few seconds. What storm of thoughts carries him away toward Yacine? Does my presence bother him, too? How I would have liked to have found myself here alone.

Another man, Paul Challes, comes to me from even farther away. Suddenly, my ears are filled with the sound of Callas's voice, Schubert's lieder, and Mozart. The medications couldn't do anything for me, nothing against the mental anorexia and the pain of solitude. As an adolescent, I had the good fortune to have a doctor who was a music enthusiast and a poet. He acted as a snake charmer, succeeding for a while in neutralizing the reptiles who nested in my fallow lands. During my vacations, during all my free moments, or black ones, I sought his wife and him out. Jeanne was a midwife. She reigned over a rotunda and multitudes of big bellies that incessantly returned to the same state. Complaints and wails, vomiting sexes. In the cries of birth I seemed to hear the screams of death. I escaped to the other wing of the hospital. I took refuge with Paul. He dictated prescriptions to me. I wrapped wounds on his instructions. With patients whom I suspected of carelessness I insisted on his orders . . . I blended myself in with his intensity. The pain and cries of others calmed me.

When work was finished, he and Jeanne took me home with them here. They had lunch while listening to music, they drank tea and ate cakes and crêpes given to them by their patients. I dined on music without tea or cakes. Music filled me up. It charmed my reptiles to sleep. It breathed its shape and its movement into my inner desert.

Often, Paul Challes would also read us poems: Rilke, Rimbaud, Nerval, Saint-John Perse. I particularly enjoyed hearing 'Winds,' by the last:

There were great winds on every surface of this world,
Very great jubilant winds throughout the
world that had neither a place to go nor a home . . .[1]

I was immediately drawn in. I was the speck of sand that, pulled into this vast drunkenness, flies and scoffs at the parched earth of the desert. I was the dead twig that begins singing again. I was the drop of sea foam carried away on a typhoon's delirium . . . The first of my appetites came

1. C'étaient de grands vents sur toutes faces de ce monde,
De très grands vents en liesse par le
monde qui n'avaient d'aire ni de gîte . . .

to me through the sense of hearing. Sounds, voices, silence, and the wind forced their way through my blocked ears, injected lungfuls of air into me and saved me. So, in spite of the unconquerable nausea that I felt about life, in spite of the craziness still gripping onto the periphery of my repulsion, this tenacious rapport with daily events anchored me to survival, to the borders of reality, for a very long time.

'What are you doing there looking like a lost dog? Give me that.'

Salah relieves me of the suitcase that I'm still carrying against my chest. I stand there like an idiot, my arms hanging down at my sides, rooted to the middle of the room. I lift my head toward the wall across from me. A fresco covers it almost entirely. It's been bothering me since I came in. I take two steps toward it. Two steps into a red blurredness. I look at the fresco without seeing it. My eyes are elsewhere, in the dense emotion flooding me.

'Why did they bury him here?'

'Where would you have liked them to bury him?' retorts Salah, surprised by my question.

'They could have buried him in Oran. He loved Oran so much.'

'Since your departure, he hadn't quit crisscrossing the desert. He'd fallen in love with it. Anyway, here or elsewhere, what difference does it make! He's no longer here.'

'This house brought together two of the men who counted the most for me.'

'Hmm, brought together? Why did you leave Yacine if he was so important to you? I've never understood anything about your story.'

They all have only this word in their mouths: to understand. How can you explain what derives from mystery? Before Yacine, I looked without seeing. I had put my eyes, covered with a tenacious film of melancholy, onto the scrap heap, in the attic of my outcasts, for such a long time that my eyes were like two pieces of fruit rotted on their branch. I don't know by what chance I found them one day at the bottom of Yacine's eyes. Immersed in his, they rubbed themselves, cleaned themselves of abstinence, of blind absence, the absence of all that is for me like a hole in nothingness. My eyes returned to me with sparkles of joy on a shining surface of arrogance. With unknown shivers. Finally, with a possible hope, though still without a goal. Before Yacine I could only tolerate the night. Night that erased the day's disasters. The darkroom night where I tried to develop the film of imprecise dreams so as to escape from the shame and the guilt of having stayed alive. From out of Yacine's eyes came light, without my having looked for it. Then the sky rose up, unfurled like a symphony: the dawn trembled like a resolving chord in a nacreous instant. The zenith's diamonds exploded into fireworks. The sunset's violins stretched out their sighs until desire blazed. The moon's laughter blew away the stars. Touching Yacine's skin, I came to know my own, his vigor and his seed heretofore hidden, pleasure's long discharges and short-circuits. Maybe we'd relearned to see together or one through the other, like two very sick people who have slowly come back to life through the same vision. Now I believe this was so. Since then, it hasn't mattered if the other were far away; he was always there in that state of attention itself, only drawn toward living in the liberated moment. Since then, from the depths of my fears, I have seen the world through the light of Yacine's eyes.

'Yacine had told me that you didn't often answer questions.'

'For him, questions were never but a twitching of his eyes. I think this reserve was what made our friendship strong.'

'Are you able to talk about your childhood now?'

'No.'

'Yacine settled here to paint the desert and to try to make you return. He used to say "to heal." I think he would have ended up discovering some things about your past.'

I turn toward him. He's opened the glass door onto the balcony. His back against the railing, he watches my reactions intently. I remain impassive.

'Why did you leave him?' he repeats.

'I had just been reborn and I felt, suddenly, such a great hunger for life . . . Little by little, Algeria's threats and restrictions became so frightening to me. So I fled from everything. An irrational flight when I felt other nightmares dawning.'

[35]

'How should your silence be interpreted?'

'As answers. As open or closed defenses, depending.'

'I think you're a woman of excess.'

'A woman of excess? Is the feeling of nothingness an excess? I'm more in between the two, on a fractured line between the two, in the midst of all ruptures. Between modesty and disdain that erodes my rebellions. Between the tension resulting from refusal and the dispersion resulting from liberties. Between the alienation caused by anguish and escape through dreams and the imagination. In an in-between place searching for its connections between the south and the north, its markers in two cultures.'

'You talk like a book. You're giving a lecture! You see, you're a woman of excess: silence or a long tirade. The Westerners have contaminated you with their tchatche and their highbrow poses.'[1]

'I have yards and yards ready of that particular tirade. And you know, this place in between permanently simmers in my head.'

'How did you learn of his death? I didn't have your number, but I knew how to find it here. Just a while ago in the plane, I wondered whether I was going to tell you. I might not have. In spite of Yacine's certainty, I thought he meant nothing to you. That was the only way I could explain your behavior to myself.'

Yacine's 'certainties' are good for me. Really good. So is the trembling doubt smothering Salah's voice.

'I called Yacine the day after his death.'

He looks at me with unbelieving eyes. Then, as if this revelation were intolerable, he turns his back on me and leans his elbows on the railing, facing the palm grove.

As for myself, I go back toward the wall. I see the fresco: a sea of flames. An agitated sea. Where the flames are unfolding a bit of smoke escapes from one. The sky is covered. A woman, seen from behind, walks unharmed on the flames. Behind her she leaves a flat white furrow like a road drawn in the fire's heavy swell. One can make out only her smoky

1. *Tchatche:* gossip.

silhouette, like a shadow play. Yacine entitled this painting *The Algerian Woman*. His signature at the bottom seems to be leaning in the margin, waiting or abandoned.

But quiet sobs tear me away from the violence of this painting. Salah's shaking tears move me. I go toward him. His back seems enormous. His convulsions fascinate me. I stare at him, not daring to touch him. When I finally manage to, he turns around abruptly, takes me in his arms and sobs even more.

'How is it that you called him on that very day?'

'I don't know. Insomnia. Autumn blues. Loneliness. A strong wind. What you might call happenstance.'

'Not a premonition?'

'Premonition? Nonsense! Nostalgia and the desire to see Yacine had been eating at me for a long time. In fact, that desire has never left me. I put it aside. I drowned it in other, more immediate desires. It always resurfaced . . . I'd received a note from him a few days earlier.'

'I hate you for everything you did to him. I hate your perverted so-called love. A fussy French-style love.'

'Oh yeah? And what's Algerian-style love like?'

'Algerian-style love? Macache! Macache![1] It's been relegated to the sinner's gallows. But you, the free woman, your love is heartless, all cerebral. You say you live only through your senses? Oualou![2] Even your silence is calculated, calibrated. A Western woman's behavior! You don't know how to talk like real Algerians. We talk in order to say nothing, we drivel on to kill time, to try to escape from boredom. For you, boredom is elsewhere. Boredom is others. You have self-important silences, silences of affluence. Silences full of books, movies, intelligent thoughts, opulence, egotism . . . Us, our starving dreams eat at us. We hug each other against the walls, and we spend our time criticizing only to hold out in an Algeria that is fasting, the prey of all demons, behind its lice-infested beard. You, you

1. *Macache:* nothing.
2. *Oualou!:* damn it all!

[37]

devoured Yacine; even when absent you had an extraordinary power over his life and his painting. At the same time you were his debt and his IMF, his arrogant north who banned him to the south, to the desert of your indifference.[1] I hate you for having been here only to bury him. You returned only to prove yourself in a place and in mourning, both of which are not yours! I hate everything that you are!'

He hiccups these words, in total discordance with his voice that seems to pray, with his arms squeezing me until I hurt. I try unsuccessfully to free myself from him. His is the true distress of a child.

'Here you are giving me a lecture, you too,' I say ironically.

He shrugs his shoulders. His tears wet my cheek. His arms hold me captive. I stroke his back to calm him. I'm rocked in his embrace and in his pain. Behind him, my eyes discover the garden, its palm trees, its aloe plants that burst out of the sand. That pomegranate tree over there . . . I remember that Jeanne had planted it. For me. Now, it's a beautiful tree, covered with gold and blood-colored pomegranates. The pomegranate is really the most beautiful of fruits. Further away, the wadi and the palm grove, like before.

'Yacine was like me,' I say, 'a ruptured being . . . When you're like this, all of your sensations are so intensified that you always seem to be dramatizing. In the eyes of others, you're permanently ridiculous or pathetic. You find yourself so profoundly at once in life and in death, in pessimism and in vitality, in paradox and in contrast. Pain is always at the heart of your joy. Fears are its heartbeats.'

'Have you also suffered from love?'

I don't answer.

'Who is it?'

Again I am silent.

'Yacine remained my friend forever, my brother. I had such great admiration for him. Since my divorce, we spent most of our weekends together, here or in Oran. Algiers is uninhabitable.'

1. IMF: International Monetary Fund.

[38]

He calms down little by little. We don't say anything more. We simply stand there, resting one against the other. Finally he lifts up his head. Tilting it to the side, he scrutinizes my face and brings his hand to my cheek.

'Those are your tears. As for me, I never manage to cry. Another one of my excesses, no doubt.'

His hand, trembling a little, moves across my face as if it were a sculpture. I give in to it entirely. The wet yellow of his eyes causes exciting agitation. Out of our bodies glued to each other, from our looks that scrutinize each other, a dizziness arises. In spite of myself, I rest my hands on his back. The arms wrapped around me are no longer those of a child. I feel his erection against my belly. I make an effort to tear myself away from him.

'I hate you for that too,' he says, with a contorted smile.

I go back to the living room.

'Do you want a little wine?' he asks me.

'I have some whiskey in my suitcase.'

'Whiskey? An émigré's luxury!'

I go to look for it, and Salah brings some glasses.

'On the black market, a bottle of whiskey costs around a thousand dinars, a third of a minimum-wage salary. Note that the Algerian never has a glass, but he gets drunk nonetheless. So it's better that he falls back on some bar. There, his wallet is at less risk. Furthermore, with almost no exception, Algerian wine is nothing but rotgut. We're the kings of self-destruction and regression.'

'And of hating women!'

He laughs nervously. 'Yes, above all, of poisoning ourselves at the source. We haven't stopped killing Algeria inch by inch, woman by woman. The male students of my generation, the elites, zaama, participated in the carnage.[1] At first we lost ourselves in lies and deception. Our Mao-style clothes and the revolutionary slogans we spat out were phony!

---

1. *Zaama:* an interjection expressing derision.

Once our studies were finished, we put them aside, threw them to the mites with our cloth legends. We abandoned those women at the university who had been imprudent enough, unfortunate enough to love us. What had they come looking for? The debauchery of knowledge. At the end of our studies, we, the young men from 'the best families,' our virility glorified by the despair of the women we'd abandoned, we threw on the traditional burnooses to sample the uncultivated virgins that our families had chosen for us. But as soon as the celebratory tambourines quieted down, our young wives seemed to us insipid and simpleminded. So we fled from our homes. We haunted bars, lived in cowardice, and some of us haunted even the most loathsome secret recesses of our souls. We subsided into scheming and schizophrenia. We did and made everything with no love, even our children. Then, those among us who could no longer tolerate that life all fled abroad. Big deal! You know, as much as I understand why the women want to leave this damned country, I condemn just as much the elite males who do so. I find their cowardice boundless. If there's still an ounce of conscience left in them, they should return and repair what they allowed to happen, since they were not affected, since the deprivations and the barbarisms strangled only the women. They should return to finally confront our gangrenous mentality. Fortunately, there were a few exceptions among us. Yacine was one of them.'

'And you?'

'Me, I behaved like an idiot. Twenty years ago I abandoned the woman who loved me for a marriage arranged by my family. I divorced a few months ago after having worked toward the unhappiness of everyone, starting with my own.'

'I find you harsh. Before I left Algeria at the end of the seventies, there were more and more students marrying each other.'

'Hmmm.'

'And you, between the abandonment of your love and your divorce with convention, how do you manage now with this "hatred" of women?'

'I cultivate it vigilantly. Our diplomas, our clothing were supposed to be signs of our modernity. But in fact, misogyny clung to us in everything we did not admit. Now I talk about it and I denounce it. But it's hardly easy to rid yourself of prejudices that seized you in the larval stage, in your mother's lap, with her milk, her voice, her attentive joy.'

For a moment he shuts himself off in serious thought. I avoid looking at him. All of a sudden he is so close to me because of his fragility, his questioning of things, and his unexpected desire. The whiskey puts my ideas back into place. My eyes explore the room. Leaning against the wall, a few paintings. Enraged sunsets and palm trees more or less splattered with mud. Berber themes and objects . . . Alone in a corner, the portrait of a little girl. Her almond-shaped eyes lend her features a dreamy surprised look. In the black of her hair, which curls like mine, a tiny star is visible like a prophet lit up by the dream consuming the star. Behind her the sky is a runny blue color.

'That's Dalila. Yacine adored that child. We're going to have to let her know about his death. I don't know how to go about it. Will you come with me?'

I agree to. What does Dalila dream about? With what mirage is she able to fight boredom? What does she know about death?

'Are your parents buried here?'

'Give me a cigarette, please.'

Somebody knocks at the door. Salah gets up and opens it. It's Khaled, coming to invite us to the funeral dinner. In spite of his kindness and insistence, I have no wish to move from here.

'Go ahead, Salah, if you want to. As for me, I'm exhausted. I got up at the crack of dawn. I feel incapable of confronting anyone. I'm staying here.'

'I'm going to help Khaled carry the platters of couscous to the mosque, and then I'm returning.'

'Oh, there are enough people at the house for that. I only wanted both of you to be with us.'

'In that case, pardon me, Khaled, but I'm going to stay here too.'

Salah lets himself drop onto a bench. Khaled hesitates, looks at us, and concludes, disappointed, 'Well, then, I'm going to have some couscous brought to you. Good night. I'll see you tomorrow.'

'Will you have a whiskey before you go?'

'No, thank you, not tonight.'

He leaves. The night is falling slowly on the palm grove. Sitting on the couch, I can see the tops of the palm trees and the sky darkening.

'Why are you having prayers said for Yacine? You know very well that he was an atheist.'

'Yes, but if I hadn't, no one would have understood.'

'So?'

'Khaled and the other poor devils would have taken up a collection to offer him what they think is owed to the dead.'

'So?'

'I didn't want that, if only because of their lack of money.'

The platter of couscous remains practically untouched. We help ourselves to some more whisky. The alcohol deadens all my feelings. It's night now. The illicitness of our situation comes suddenly to mind. A man and a woman, two strangers under the same roof. The honor of the village is in danger tonight. It's the first return to transgression. That suits me. Salah turns on the light.

'I'm going to make the bed for you in Yacine's room. Me, I'll sleep on the couch. I'm used to it.'

I take a pill so I'll sink quickly into sleep. All evening, I'd made sure that I didn't go into Yacine's room, didn't discover this bed where death was waiting, like a traitor, to snatch him up. 'In perfect health'? For three years the thread of my imagination has been focused on this bed. In the thread of my thoughts, a silent film started over and over again, obsessively.

Lying down on my stomach, leaning on my elbows, the receiver in my hand, Yacine talks to me. I don't hear him.

Salah is sitting on the ground, his back against the wall, his knees pulled up toward his chest. He's telling about his life in Algiers, the progressive deterioration of working conditions at the hospital, the daily violence of the FIS that remind him of the OAS's wrongdoings, the lack of certitude for the future.[1] My mind wanders through the house, the garden, and into the palm grove. If I'd had the strength to do so, I would have gone for a walk in the gardens bordering the wadi. The sky is of sparkling velvet, hung on the glass door. Every so often I seem to feel another's eyes on me. I don't dare find it, affront it, or analyze the effect it has on me.

I turn my attention again to Salah's voice. I begin listening to his narration again. I fall asleep under his protection. But I wake up with a start when he tries to carry me into the bedroom.

'Wait, wait, I'm going.'

I close the door. Lying flat on his stomach, his torso propped up on his elbows, Yacine smiles at me. A folded blanket is placed at the foot of the bed. I close my eyes. I move toward the blanket, bend down and get it. I unfold it next to the bed and stretch out on it. I keep my eyes closed. Yacine's hands, mouth, and body immediately take hold of mine.

'Sultana, Sultana!'

Salah is leaning over me.

'What's going on?'

'Wake up. It's two o'clock in the afternoon!'

I sit up. All my muscles are cramped and stiff.

'If I'd known that you were going to sleep on the floor, I would have left you on the sofa . . . is something the matter?'

1. OAS: Organisation armée secrète, partisans of keeping Algeria French, who planned and carried out terrorist acts.

'Last night I made love to Yacine.'

'If you sleep on the floor like that, don't be surprised if you have night-mares afterward!'

'But . . . it wasn't a nightmare.'

'What do you mean?'

'It wasn't a nightmare . . . it was nice. As soon as I crossed the thresh-old Yacine was here in the room. He was waiting for me.'

'You were sleeping standing up. You know quite well that it isn't possi-ble! Yesterday afternoon we buried Yacine!'

'I wasn't sleeping. I swear to you that . . .'

'Stop it, Sultana! Come on now!'

My body is like worm-eaten wood. I can't move. Salah takes me around my waist and pushes me toward the bathroom.

'Go on, take a shower, that'll wake you up. What did you take to sleep yesterday? As upset as you were, the fatigue, the alcohol, and a sleeping pill . . . you must have hallucinated! Anyway! You're a doctor, you know about these things . . . Coffee or tea?'

'Coffee . . . coffee, please.'

'And fried eggs and the oranges and dates that Khaled gathered for you this morning.'

'Did you see him?'

'Yes, we went to the souk together, then to the cemetery for the sadaka . . .[1] When he discovered that you were also a doctor, Khaled suggested that you fill in temporarily for Yacine. He's crazy! I didn't think it was use-ful to tell him that you were from here. In any case, he doesn't seem to have recognized you.'

'You were right to do that . . . Yacine's job?'

'You're not going to do that, are you?'

'Why not? Just until there's another candidate for the job. And anyway, I'd like to stay here a few days.'

'Months and months could go by before . . .'

1. *Sadaka:* alms.

[44]

'Listen, I'm going to think about it.'

'No, no, not here. You can't imagine how difficult life is in this part of the world, even for a man. All of those who don't conform are swiftly, radically, and permanently banished.'

'Believe me, I know.'

He stares at me, alarmed, and ends up dropping the subject.

'I'll let you take a shower. I'm going to make breakfast.'

He leaves. Standing in front of the mirror, I look at myself. My face is distorted and there are bags under my eyes. Who is she, this woman with her sickening pout, and such tired eyes?

'Salah!'

'Yes.'

'Did you shave this morning?'

'No, not yet. I woke up feeling guilty about Khaled. I left quickly to go look for him. Why?'

'The razor is all wet.'

'I must have splashed it while I was washing. Good God, Sultana, get these morbid ideas and that crap out of your head!'

I hear his steps in the hallway and his angry voice: 'Go on, hop in the shower!'

He comes in, pushes me, and turns on the faucet.

'If you're not out of there in three minutes, I'll come back and get you,' he warns me before leaving.

I look at my sopping wet T-shirt sticking to my skin little by little. I end up taking it off and dropping it underfoot. The water slides over my skin like a hand.

Somebody bangs on the door just when we're getting ready to go out. Bakkar crosses the threshold, peremptorily pushes Salah aside with his hand, and moves toward me. Now I completely recognize his features invaded by a thick beard. Bakkar, village mayor! Do people have to fall into such deep blindness? Does Algeria have to be so tainted so that only the humble, the crooks, and the violent triumph?

[45]

'I am the mayor,' he says, overflowing with self-satisfaction.

I look at him and have the worst time staying serious. His eyes ferret about across the dining room, stop at the whiskey bottle and the two glasses left on the table. Horrified, they return to me with all the world's condemnation and start to poke around again. He twists his neck, contorts himself to try to see inside the bedroom.

'What do you want?'

'I am the mayor!' He screams 'I am the mayor' as if to say 'Watch out!' I unabashedly burst out laughing.

'What do you want?'

'I don't want any of this here! This is a state employee's house, not a brothel!'

'What do you want?'

'You, who are you?'

'A friend of Doctor Yacine Meziane.'

'But who are you?'

'That's none of your business.'

'You're lucky that I need you. Otherwise I would have sent over the police.'

'Why the police?'

'Prostitution!'

'Oh, really? Why do you say that?'

'You drink alcohol and you sleep with him!' he says haughtily, indicating Salah with his head.

'And why do you need me?'

'The nurse told me you're a doctor. I need a doctor for the village. But you have to show me your papers and your degrees and stay quiet.'

'I won't show you anything at all. As for the job, if you'd behaved properly, I would have maybe tried to do something.'

'Me, not proper? And you're the one insulting me?'

'Take it as you like!'

'If you refuse to be the doctor I'll send over the police!'

Salah grabs him. 'That's enough of your threats! Get out of here!'

'Saturday morning at nine o'clock, you come to my office,' he cries out at me, and addressing Salah, 'and you, don't you stay here! You go home and don't you come back!'

'Get out of here!'

He disappears.

'You who wanted to stay, have you seen enough of what they're capable of?'

'I know that they're capable of even worse.'

4

VINCENT

The sky here is unique. It's so big, so engulfing, that everywhere you feel surrounded by it, as if you're flying when you're simply walking. You feel like a speck of dust in frothy light, the sun's dust drunken with reflections. Or maybe a playful sylph leaving, sucked in by an immense sky blue dream. But I want to feel all these sensations without mysticism or eroticism. For just the right amount of time. Just what I need for my joy.

I walk in the streets. I lose myself in the overcrowded neighborhoods. I melt into the crowd of children. They trail after me. Their feet bare. Their looks bare. Their words bare. I stop. They jostle each other, squabble, discuss, group together, and assail me with laughter and questions. I answer them. I lose myself and catch myself again. They make fun of me. Sometimes volleys of words, deliciously treacherous, pierce their innocence. The words go by. Angels return to settle onto their foreheads. A little further, their curiosity worn out, they pass me on to others as if I were a toy. A toy that plays. I continue on my way.

The adults greet me, smile at me. I'm an attraction. An adolescent boy follows on my footsteps, acts as interpreter when necessary, imposes his exclusive protection on me. By the end of the afternoon he's managed to ward off all the other assaults of sympathy. By the end of the afternoon we're alone, like brothers. A despotic brother, he harasses me, loses patience, and commands me to go 'eat at the house.' Absolutely not! I resist and instead invite him to eat out. Already more than once in the Barbès and Belleville districts, I felt obligated to give in to these imperious and impromptu invitations for which the North Africans have the secret. But can you eat a succulent couscous or a tajine without wine?[1] That seems sacrilegious to me, I who have no religion. For a while I found myself confronted by the following dilemma: home cooking, simmered in the feminine tradition, with the eternal lemonade, or a boring dish, improved by some wine, when the restaurant business is nothing but a last resort, masculine, a North African source of income. No sacrifice at all. A little extra spice and I can easily give up a little quality for more permissiveness. Gazouz?[2] Very little for me. Gascon, Christian, and atheist by my father; Jewish by my mother, Polish and practicing out of solidarity; North African through my transplant and with no borders, through a 'tissue identity,' I nevertheless have gregarious and stubborn habits. My identity gathers nectar according to its own will, makes its honey, and crosses one old tannin with another. It mixes, accommodates. I don't reject anything. I'm an eclectic, a harlequin, as Michel Serres would say.[3] It's certain that my Jewish fibers, for example, are a little trimmed. But I value them! On Saturdays I turn on the stove only to make my morning coffee. I never cook. I go out to eat what I like. Couscous? Yes, yes. I like that, and thanks to my kidney I have a crossbred alimentary environment. It's got to be reciprocal assimilation! To eat only French food would be pure colonization. Beware of rebellions and my body's rejection of the organ. How is it that racists, penetrated to the inmost depths of the intestines by foreign foods (and to their own satisfaction), don't lower their guard? That the flavor of dishes induces no sympathy among gourmets remains a mystery to me. The tongue that has learned to savor the taste of cinna-

1. *Tajine:* a meat or vegetable stew cooked in a specially shaped earthenware pot.
2. *Gazouz:* lemonade made with carbonated water.
3. Michel Serres: French philosopher, professor at the Sorbonne and Stanford University. Member of the French Academy.

mon, carvil, coriander, or ginger, can also rant and rave unrestrainedly about 'the noises and smells' that surround them.[1] It's a matter of stomach! Alas, cooking does not have the virtues of the cocktail medications used to prevent a transplanted organ from being rejected. Cooking doesn't make the body more tolerant.

Anyway. Now I know. Now, when I don't know people, I only give in to tea. I take my precautions for a meal. Besides, my companion is delighted. It's the first time that he's eaten out.

'Do you have any wine?' he asks the waiter for me.

'No, I don't, but for the roumi I'll ask my friend.[2] He'll go get some.'

He goes out and after a second returns with a bottle hidden in a dirty rag. It's uncorked.

'That's all there is,' warns the cheap restaurant owner.

Take it or leave it. I serve a glass of it to my companion. At the first sip he makes a face but continues anyway. After a moment, his swarthy face becomes wine colored.

'The wine is going to drip from the end of your nose and your ears,' I joke.

He smiles blissfully at me.

'Here, men always hide to get drunk.'

'So you're breaking with custom?' A mischievous laugh. After he glances around he exclaims, 'There's no one!'

The wine is mediocre and the food edible. At the end of the meal, Moh (the chic name for Muhammad, he proudly explains to me) writhes about and stammers with confusion, finally confessing that he would like to take me with him to the brothel. My refusal makes him red with anger, redder than wine.

'What? You aren't normal? You haven't had enough to drink?'

Well, no, I'm not entirely normal. But I keep that to myself. I'm also not

1. Carvil: a spice related to cumin.
2. *Roumi:* Christian.

going to admit to him my desire to go admire the sky, alone. So I mention my fear of AIDS. AIDS? *He* doesn't give a damn. Rubbers? The same.

'AIDS only gets people who fuck from behind and who've got sick Western morals!' he objects sententiously.

'So what are "sick Western morals"?' I ask naively.

'You, you lick all over, even down below like dogs! We, we do it clean, fast and right. And anyway, rubbers are for people who have one with a fragile head. Mine, mine is honest to God, a desperado. May Allah protect it!'

This boy astonishes and exhausts me. I've had my dose of him for this evening. I give the excuse that I'm dropping from lack of sleep. And to make sure I get rid of him, I accompany my young buck to his destination. With the eye of a conqueror, he hurls a scornful goodnight at me and rushes into the temple, swaggering like a boxer going into the ring. Whew, I'm free!

I return slowly to the hotel. It's not even nine o'clock and the few cafés have already closed. I feel like I'm walking through a ghost town. A few streetlight halos bore into and disrupt the night. Children and adolescents gather around them. Ghostly gandouras step out of the light and melt into the darkness.[1] Others burst suddenly into the light. Above the streetlights, bats fly round and round without stopping. Sometimes I walk past men strolling, holding each others' hands. This type of masculine body contact gives them a singular look, in a night in pain, deprived of women. The total absence of women creates this feeling of unreality. I'll never get used to it! In a hurry, busy, they go through the day, the time to cross a street, the time for some courage, between two markers of the forbidden. The evening swallows all of them up. Stone walls or earthen walls, walls of fears and of censure bury them. I despair. The Algerians argue endlessly, sinking into boredom.

---

1. *Gandoura:* a sleeveless article of clothing worn underneath a burnoose.

Protected by the night, I pass by unnoticed for now. I feel peace. I'm going to go have something to drink at the hotel and afterward I'll go sit on the dunes. The whole day I thought often of Dalila. I take the street where I saw her disappear this morning. Which of these houses is hers? And the teacher's? They're all closed up. As one goes farther from the center the silence thickens. Will Dalila be on the dunes tomorrow? I have to go see this famous Yacine.

I see her as soon as I cross the threshold of the hotel lounge. As I enter, she moves suddenly. Disappointed, her eyes immediately abandon me. I call them back, beg them to give me their charm again. They disregard me. Who is she? For whom is she waiting? A man is sitting across from her. Chestnut-colored hair, elegantly dressed. Very aware of the changes of expression on her face, he observes me with a jaundiced eye. They exchange a few words. Maybe about me. It doesn't matter that I've gotten suntanned on the boat – my blond hair and blue eyes tell everyone I'm foreign. The mixed part inside me can't be seen, and I can't brandish my scars or my HLA cartography to show my universality.[1] She is the only woman. Thin, chocolate-colored skin, curly coffee-colored hair like Dalila's, with an ardent mystery in her eyes. Looking elsewhere, a look from elsewhere, that flashes without seizing anything; a look that makes me tremble. In what deep puzzle could I be tracking her? Her disenchanted pout stopped me and froze me in my tracks. I do violence to myself if I try to detach my eyes from her. I look around me. The other men are looking at her, too, are looking only at her. Could it be any other way? In the men's eyes, fear, condemnation, admiration, desire, and questioning cross each other and weigh down the atmosphere, burden their voices that have become only intermittent whispers. She drinks a beer with little gulps, automatically wiping her lips with the back of her hand. She is

1. HLA: Human leucocyte antigen, a system of tissue typing, the equivalent of blood typing.

so far gone in what is strange and different, so alone in what she lacks. She is a challenge.

I sit down at a table where I can admire her as I wish. I order a beer. I am the only one here who slept in the hotel last night. The other men who were there, probably executives and merchants, all returned to the city. The Sonatour Hotel is the only place where these men can meet and drink alcohol.

The woman gets up and goes toward the door. The man follows her. The room goes quiet. The bartender stops what he was doing. The air becomes electrified. I would not want to be a woman in this country. I would not want to have to permanently carry the burden of these looks, their many forms of violence, sharpened by frustration. For the first time, I realize that an Algerian woman's most ordinary act is, from the beginning, charged with symbols and heroism, because masculine animosity is so great, so pathological. The atmosphere is intolerable to me. I would have liked to have gone up to the dune. I don't dare leave immediately after them. I take my beer with me and ask for the key to my room.

I don't turn on the light. I open the glass door. The view of the sky dispels my malaise. The outline of the palm trees, the curve of their fronds in the charcoal-colored night, the moon's milky light on the highest tips of the palm grove, and the air's balminess all mix their softness. At the foot of the dune, two cigarettes glowing in the dark attract my attention. When my eyes become accustomed to the darkness, I can make out two silhouettes. It's definitely them. They're sitting on the sand. It isn't long before the other customers have left the hotel lounge and are scattered outside spying on them. Once they've located the couple, their heads turn frequently toward them. In the name of God, why can't they leave them the hell alone!

Over on the dune the cigarettes go out. The woman and man return to the hotel. After a moment, I hear their voices in the hallway. The man's voice is begging her. I don't understand what she is saying. One door slams. I hear a few steps and a second one squeaks lightly. Then silence closes in on these second-floor rooms.

Downstairs, the men leave, one after another. A few by car, most on foot.

I feel dirty. Dirty, sad, and irritated. I'm going to take a shower, rub my body down with soap. Then I'll bury myself in some poetry. Right now, I feel incapable of reading a novel.

The shower head refuses to work. The sink's faucet farts, burps, and doesn't yield a single drop. My friends had warned me that the plumbing here was a capricious and greedy ventriloquist. I'd believed their warnings to be exaggerated, so much was I suspicious of all the French clichés about Algeria. I go downstairs to try to find a solution. There's no one. Only three keys are missing from the board. The night watchman and the guard have disappeared. I go back upstairs, taking care not to make any noise. As I reach my door the faint sound of a hiccup reaches my ears. I freeze and listen. Somebody is crying softly but the rooms are so badly insulated . . . I retrace my steps. It's coming from room 15. A man's sob. I'm dying to tap at that door. I hold myself back. I return to my room.

Stretched out on my bed, I think about these two strangers, my neighbors on this floor. I think about the man's sadness. Is she the cause of it? I can't help feeling a little joy, knowing that they're in two different rooms. Am I stupid? I know nothing about her, nor about him. I try to chase her out of my mind, to plunge into Rilke's 'Orchards': 'This voice, almost mine, rises, deciding no longer to return.' Through the wide-open glass door, the sky's evening blue enhances my daydreaming.

When I awaken the sun has been up for a long time. Already eight o'clock! I've never slept this long. Even the muezzin didn't disturb my sleep. I'm settling into local customs. My transplant? It hasn't moved. The fist of a little sisterly hand holding on to my guts. Bud of my dreams under the scars of my identity. I caress it. It reassures me. The sky is radiant.

It takes me some time to make out Dalila. She's stretched out at the top of the dunes. Why isn't she at school? What day is it? Saturday. Yes, Saturday. Yet it's the first day of the week here.

The faucet is still just as dry. Dry and now mute. I go down to the front desk to ask for water. A boy gives me a bucketful and promises to leave me some in reserve in my room.

'Water is inch'Allah here, like everything else,' he says, looking sorry.[1]

Like everything else. Going back up the stairs, I remember that at the hotel where I'd slept in Oran, a young man traveling, worried about an important rendezvous in Algiers, had described Air Algeria as 'Air Inch'Allah.'

As I approach, Dalila sits down and stares at me dismally. What's happened to her? Her eyes are red and her features upset.

'Don't bother going to Aïn Nekhla! Yacine's dead,' she thrusts at me in a desperate tone of voice, before I've reached the top.

Astonishment glues me to the spot.

'What, dead?'

'Dead! Dead, dead is all!'

'Oh, shit!'

'I thought it was his car. He always said, "It's going to give up the ghost." But he's the one who died, and so did his soul with him.'

'But what did he die of?'

'Nothing, he just died. It isn't the Islamists who killed him. He died all alone, in his sleep.'

'Well, shit! How old was he?'

'Yeah, shit is right! Well, shit!' she repeats in a rage, without managing to console herself.

'How old was he?'

'How old is he . . . like you. You, how old are you?'

'Forty years old.'

'Like you, I'm sure.'

1. *Inch'Allah:* according to the will of God.

[55]

We go quiet. A stunned silence.

Her eyes are glued to me. Her eyes pierce me. Through the cloth of my pants pocket, my hand looks for my kidney, a comfort.

'When you're always alone, is it like an illness? Like a cancer that kills?'

'No, not him. His work must have interested him a lot, and anyway, from what you told me, painting filled his whole life.'

'Is painting a space?'

'Yes, a rich space.'

'Me, I think that Ouarda, the professor, she tells the truth. People who always stay alone, they all catch space sickness, like Yacine, like my sister, Samia, like Salah, Yacine's friend, who told me about his death, like the woman who came with him, yesterday. Her face is like someone who has space in her head and who wants more. Like you too?'

'Who's Salah?'

'In LaFrance, I dunno, but here it's not normal to stay alone. With us, the only space is family. Yacine, he doesn't have a wife. He doesn't have a child. He doesn't have a family. All he does is work and draw.'

'Who's Salah?'

'His friend. He's a doctor too. Aren't you listening to me? He's the one who came and told me about his death.'

'What's Salah like?'

'He has yellow eyes. He's Kabyle too. He's at the hotel. You didn't see him?'

'Oh, yes, yes . . . Do you know the woman who's with him?'

'No. Salah, he came with Yacine. Her, I don't know her. Her face is like the ones who walk and don't want to be like the others. Yacine, he could marry her, since she's a friend of his. But her face is like ones who stay alone, her too.'

'Was he buried?'

'Look, it's them.'

The man and the woman come out of the hotel each carrying a little suitcase. The car starts, disappears into the town. Won't I see her anymore? I don't even know her name. My melancholy grows stronger.

'They put him in a hole and now they leave and go home with his car.'

'When did they bury him?'

'Yesterday in Aïn Nekhla.'

'Was he kind of like a big brother to you?'

'Yes, but not like the brothers that I have, like a brother I'd like to have . . . Why do people always tell lies about death?'

'What lies?'

'They always say that dead people go to heaven, to the sky.'

'Because they believe that. Does that shock you?'

'Dead people stay in the earth. They don't go to the sky. If all the dead people were in the sky, it'd be black with people, even blacker than when there's locusts! When my dog died, my dad went to bury him over there. After two weeks I went to the tomb and I dug. I wanted to see. My dog's skin was all full of worm holes. Full, full of worms, and it smelled bad, so bad that I couldn't even cry. All I did was throw up on my dog's body, and my throwing up and my dog, it was the same thing. Then I couldn't stop anymore . . . Afterward I was sick and I had nightmares. That's all death is. Heaven, it's just a nest of worms, a trap of rotten earth for catching people's lives, and they always fall in.'

'You say that because you're sad. But the idea of paradise is a space that helps a lot of people live. Not everyone has the same concept of it that you have.'

'Paradise isn't a space! It's a death trap. Inside it, life becomes throwing up. Death, death's true. It's in the earth. You can't dream well with what's true. To dream, you need things that don't exist and things from the sky, not the earth.'

'You dream a lot on your dune, you do. You dream about her sometimes, don't you?'

'First of all, sand isn't made of earth. Sand, there's sun in it. I tell myself that sand fell from the sun. It isn't from the earth. Sand makes light and sparkles. Earth just makes mud or dust. In the summer you can walk barefoot on the earth. You can't do that on sand. You'd burn your feet. And sand moves, it goes everywhere, even in your mouth and your closed eyes. The dune, it moves around. It changes shape. Sometimes, it's like the chest of a very, very fat mama, sometimes like her stomach. Sometimes like a butt or a back bent over praying. It makes shadow holes and round-shaped fire. Sometimes it trembles. Sometimes it has slippery skin. And then it flies, sand does. In the wind, it goes as far as the sky. It puts out the sky. In the wind, it travels, it cries out, it cries, it dances, it sings like Bliss.'

'Bliss?'

'Yes, Bliss is the devil from here.'

'Well, I'll say, your sand does inspire you!'

'What's that mean, "inspire you"?'

'It gives you dreams and words to say them.'

'Because the erg is the sea of dreams.'

'A sea like the Mediterranean or like the one that gives us life?'

'Both of them. Samia, she told me that the sea is an erg made of water that erases the waves. Then it becomes flat like a reg.[1] I saw it in photos and in books, the sea. The sea is like the mother of fish and also of sailors. And the sailors that are on it, they don't always see the fish that are at the bottom of the water. They don't see the salt either. The erg, it's the sea from here. And in the sand, on the sand, are the people from dreams who go to the sky and come back down, who make light, and who never die. The people from life, they don't always know how to see them. Me, I see them, I talk to them.'

'Oh, good. So I'm maybe one of those sailors?'

'No, you leave footprints when you walk. Look at your prints. People from life, they all make footprints. That's how death can watch them. Even with shoes, they're attached to earth with footprints. And then one day, death rewinds them.'

'Who's the one female who doesn't make footprints? The one that ran away when I arrived yesterday?'

She shrugs her shoulders.

---

1. *Reg:* a particular form of rocky desert.

'I won't tell you.'

'Okay, okay . . . who else do you see in dreamland?'

'When I was little, my sister Samia, she would read *The Bendir* to me.'[1]

'*The Bendir*? What's that?'

'Oh, no, in LaFrance they call it *The Tin Drum*. It also has another name that's like Omar.'

'Oscar, Oscar the Drum. Samia told you that story? It's a very beautiful book. It's been made into a film. Have you seen the film?'

'Where do you think you are? I don't have the right to go to the movies. On television there's only *Dallas*, films with war or fights, and Egyptian films, sometimes with Samia Gamal. We here in the desert, we're not "paraboled."'

'Paraboled?'

'Yes, it's when you have the antenna that hooks you up to LaFrance.'

'Okay, a satellite dish.'

'The Islamists say "paradiabolical," but they're really glad when they have it. Us, we're too far away. The government antennas don't reach us.'

'So what about *The Tin Drum*?'

'I was little and I thought the sky was a ceiling made of blue glass. The Drum came to see me on the dune. I'd always ask him to break the sky like he breaks light bulbs and window panes at home. I wanted to see what was behind. I wanted this so much that sometimes I had fits of anger. Huge fits that made me cry. The Drum cried and cried, the poor thing! But he couldn't break the sky. He said to me, "I can't because the sky isn't like a bulb or a windowpane. The sky is too big, too hard for me. If I were big, with a big cry, maybe I'd break it." But if he were big, he wouldn't have had a cry that breaks things.'

'Surely he would have, yes. Who else comes to see you from dreamland?'

'The Little Sultan. In LaFrance they call him the Little Prince. Him too, he's looking for space for his flower. I asked him to tell his friend to break

1. *Bendir:* drum.

the sky with his airplane. At first he didn't want to because of his star, which is so little, with his flower on it. And also his friend can't fly anymore because he fell into the ocean with his airplane. Samia told me. It's nice to die in the sea! Plop, from the sky you go into the great water. There aren't worms in the sea, and it makes two skies: a sky of water with colored fish and above, a sky of air with stars that maybe have love flowers.

'When I grew up, I learned that the sky is just air, always air, so much that it becomes blue with stars, which are balls of fire whirling inside. I like that a lot, to know that up there it's not closed. When I'm grown up, I'll fly airplanes that go really, really high in the stars.'

'Those are rockets. So you want to become an astronaut?'

'Yes, astro. . . ?'

'Astronaut.'

'An astronaut, yes. When they get out of their airplane, they fly in the air slowly, slowly. It's really beautiful. If I'd been big, I would have taken Yacine way up there and I would have let him go into the air. That way he would have really been in the sky. He would have always flown with the stars and the Little Prince and his flower, in a clean blue place.'

'Who else do you talk to in your dreams?'

'Also with Jaha and Targou.[1] They're from here. Targou is a dead woman who isn't really dead, who never goes to bed, who never rests. Everybody says she's mean like the devil. It's not true! She's bored being all alone in time that doesn't pass, so she plays jokes on people so she can laugh.'

'Would you like to go visit Yacine's tomb? I'll take you there if you want.'

'No, I don't want to go see his tomb. I'd think of worms and of throwing up . . . I only want to think of him standing when he draws, not lying down, not in the earth.'

She's full of held-back tears. I feel helpless in the face of her great pain. We don't say anything more.

She finally gets up.

1. Jaha: in legends, a very mischievous character. Targou: legendary female ghost.

[60]

'Are you going to school?'

'No, I'm going to a hiding place. Today I'm on strike. I don't wanna see anybody. I don't wanna go to school. I don't wanna eat. I don't wanna go home.'

'They're going to hit you, like you say.'

She shrugs her shoulders and goes slowly toward the palm grove. After a moment she turns toward me.

'Yacine should be put in a book.'

'Put in a book? You mean write something about him?'

'Yes, something pretty. That way he'll come into dreams like the Little Sultan and the Bendir. He looks like them, except he's bigger. He's not really real! Real men, they don't draw, they don't live all alone. So it must be easy to put him in a book.'

'We could try. It's difficult and it takes a long time to write a book, you know. But we can think about it.'

She takes off. Since I can't help her, I let her go.

I should leave, disappear further into the desert. My resolve fails me. It would be wonderful if I could take Dalila to the sea, this sea full of sailors and fish; let her discover navigation in a sailboat. But that's just a pipe dream.

I go round in circles in town. I buy some newspapers. I drink tea while I read them. I hadn't imagined there'd be such a great press in Algeria. All these dailies, these weeklies. Some of them mediocre, perpetuating stereotyped formal language. Others excellent, mixing spontaneity and scholarly analysis, truthfulness, humor, and fierceness, juicy verbs, a fricassee of French peppered with Algerian, mixed-breed language.

At the end of the morning, I take the car and head toward Aïn Nekhla. Gray, lifeless asphalt that, in the distance, comes to life in a swarming of metallic bursts. The road zooms past beneath me, straight and narrow. Like a steel blade, it cuts out an infinitely long reg and pierces the horizon with a spurt of light. The sky is a war-colored blue.

I enter Aïn Nekhla. A village without appeal. On my immediate right,

I pass by the hospital sign, Yacine's realm. Parked right in front, the car that Dalila had shown me that morning. I would have recognized this impossibly candy-colored pink Peugeot 204 among a thousand others. Maybe they haven't left? A shiver of joy flows all the way down my spine.

A man in white comes toward me.

'May I see a doctor, please?'

'You're lucky, sir. First of all, because no one else is waiting; this morning I sent away all the patients because there wasn't a doctor. Second, because we've had a doctor again for an hour. El hamdoulillah![1] Sit down there for a moment. She's doing the hospital rounds.'

She? This 'she' knocks me off my feet. I sit down on the cement bench. Is it she? The man, probably a nurse, leaves me. A cavernous silence envelops me. A dreadful silence that tramples me . . . How long did I spend waiting for her? A long time.

Steps in the corridor. There she is. She. She, drowned in an oversized doctor's coat. She, cramped by an enormous rough collar. The coat's shoulders reach the middle of her arms. She's rolled up the sleeves above her elbows. She, with the same tormented eyes.

'Have I already seen you?' she asks hesitatingly.

'Last night at the Sonatour Hotel.'

'Oh, yes, that's it. What can I do for you?'

'Oh, just a simple checkup.'

'But why did you come all the way here?'

'I had promised little Dalila to visit her friend Yacine.'

'He's no longer alive . . .'

'Yes, I know. Dalila told me.'

'When did you see Dalila?'

'This morning.'

'How was she?'

'Bad, subject to feverish lucidity interrupted by dreams. She announced to me that she's on strike about everything.'

1. *El hamdoulillah:* Mercy on us.

'On strike about everything?'

'Eating, going to school, home . . .'

'Last night, when we told her about Yacine's death, she collapsed onto the sand. Then she got up and went toward the palm grove without a word. I wanted to run after her to console her. Salah, the friend who was with me, held me back . . . He told me she's always alone, a bit wild.'

'Alone, yes, wild, no. She's running away from a certain number of things. She's invented a world and is taking refuge in it.'

'Will you see her again?'

'Yes, at least I hope so.'

'I'd like to entrust you with this present for her. A painting – more precisely, a portrait, her portrait.'

'She talked to me about this portrait. There may be a little problem though. Her friend, the doctor . . .'

'Doctor Meziane. Yacine Meziane.'

'Doctor Meziane already wanted to give it to her. But she was afraid of her parents' reaction.'

'Obviously, obviously! I hadn't thought of that. I haven't found my native reflexes yet, if I ever even had any.'

'Found?'

'Yes. I've been living in France for fifteen years . . . But come, come in, please.'

'I've had a transplant. A kidney . . . I had very rare luck, the jackpot of transplants: I have a completely matched kidney.'

'Magnificent! You must have a very minimal immunosuppressant as treatment.'

'Yes, do you know something about nephrology?'

'A little . . . to tell the truth, I almost specialized in it. The heavy machinery for the artificial kidney, the prowess of kidney transplants, have greatly fascinated me for a long time. And then one day I gave it up.'

'Why?'

'Got fed up with the hospital ayatollahs. I'll be careful not to generalize. However, when they're dealing with dark-skinned people, some of

them have pontificating and scornful speech and fundamentalist atti-
tudes toward knowledge. They easily parade around in front of their terrorized yes men, who then march in step after them. As for their misogyny disguised by hypocrisy . . .'

'I believe you.'

'Lie down there,' she says, pointing to the examination table.

I take off my shirt and pants and stretch out. She examines me. I want
to imprison her hands in mine, those hands on my transplant, to keep
them there indefinitely. Her look, the expression on her face, are completely normal for now. She auscultates my kidney and concludes: 'No
murmur. Pressure thirteen over seven. No sign of vascular overload. Perfect, you can get dressed. I'll order a blood test for you.'

'Have you decided to stay here?'

'No, just long enough for the commune to find someone again.'

Everything is happening so fast, too fast.

'There, well, good-bye, Mr. Chauvet.'

I don't move.

'Could you go see Dalila?'

She seems puzzled. I try to find a convincing argument. I say, 'She has
only one sister that she hasn't seen for a long time. She stayed in France
after finishing her studies. I think it'll do her good to talk about it with
you. Dalila is in the process of discovering solitude in her erg as in the
heart of her family. She scrutinizes "those who are looking for space." '

'Those who are looking for space?'

'Yes, she'll explain it better to you than I can. She says you have "the
face of one who is looking for space and who doesn't want to live like
everyone else." '

She smiles.

'I'll go see her tomorrow at the end of the afternoon.'

She takes off her doctor's coat. Her body regains its harmony and her
look, that alarm which isolates and distances her. She prepares to leave. I
also get up.

'I'll see you tomorrow, then.'

[64]

She has already left. Tomorrow, so far away. Tomorrow, an 'inch'Allah' that's different from the others.

At the end of the day I waited for Dalila on her observatory. In vain. Is she on strike against dreams, too? The waves from the erg thicken the silence on the reg's strand. The infinite undulation of the sands sublimate escape to the point of tragic immobility. The sun sinks into red despair. A mute sob rains onto the dune.

I return to the hotel. I stay on the terrace, facing the sand's swell. I feel in me a panting from the sea, anxious, deaf waters waiting for the wind's breath. I am a sailor without a boat, the shimmering of a mirage, between sky and sand.

When I awake, I listen carefully for the muezzin's voice, my eyes still closed. Only silence. Most certainly silence. A virginal call, stronger than prayer, an intensity of life gathered, in revolt, that draws me in. I open my eyes. Dawn at my window. I see myself. What's abnormal about me on the birth of this day? My hand is on my kidney. My kidney beneath its scar. Its familiar curvature. Life fallen asleep, the presence-absence of my Siamese twin return to my memory. She came into my room through the open glass door. She wore a long white doctor's coat and the face of the doctor, a spatial figure. She caressed my kidney, my lips, my cock. I un-buttoned her coat, took her breasts in my hands. We drank from each other until delirious.

I hadn't had a hard-on, even in my dreams, for such a long time. 'That's normal, it's the illness. Don't worry about it, it'll return after the trans-plant,' the doctors endlessly repeated. They didn't reassure me. My hand makes a careful incursion to the side of my penis and pulls back immedi-ately as if burned. I throw back the sheet. I look, I see my cock. It's stand-ing up like an acanthus blooming again after months of wilt. Reanimated phallus, a life again revived by a milky dawn against the darkness of my libido.

5

SULTANA

I stayed in Aïn Nekhla. Salah's entreaties and warnings? No hold on me. He left worried. I remain in limbo. Neither the feeling of being socially useful nor the presence of my birthplace are able to pull me out of this state. I am simply here by inertia. I feel the fire of nostalgia only at a distance. Returning has killed my nostalgia and left me only with naked exile. I myself have become this exile, cut off from any attachment.

And anyway, Algeria or France, what does it matter! Archaic Algeria, with its stale lie of modernity; hypocritical Algeria, who no longer fools anyone, who would like to build for itself sham virtue by having a hypothetical 'foreign hand' shoulder all of its blunders, all of its errors; absurd Algeria, its self-mutilation and its schizophrenia; the Algeria who commits suicide each day, no matter what.

Self-important and zealous France, what does it matter, either? France, who brandishes to the world its president's prostate gland, truffle of its imperial democracy; France, who bombards children here, who offers a banana to a dying African, victim of famine, there, and who, in front of its television screens, delights in watching him die with a good conscience; pontificating France, now Tartuffe, now Machiavelli, dressed like a humanist, what does it matter?

Yes, what do countries, nations matter, what do institutions and all the abstract ideas matter when it's in the individual himself that the worm is immortal?

[66]

I had a heart attack over my Algeria. Such a long time ago. Now my heart is again pounding without pain. But an aftereffect of necrosis remains: the bucket of abandonment at the never-sealed source of blood. I'm half paralyzed over my France. Little by little, half of my body has again found its automatic functioning, recuperated its sensations. Yet a zone of my brain remains mute to me, as if not lived in: an absence lies in wait for me at the borders of my fears, at the threshold of my loneliness.

Leave again? Leave both France and Algeria? Carry to some other place the hypertrophied memory of exile? Try to find somewhere else without roots, with neither racism nor xenophobia, without warmongers? Without a doubt, this phantasmagorical country exists only in the hopes of utopians. Any refuge is precarious, as soon as one has left for the first time. Elsewhere cannot be a remedy. The differences in geography can do nothing against the constant similarity of men. How many of us will be searching somewhere else at the dawn of the year 2000? Leave or stay, what does it matter? My only real community is the community of ideas. I've never had any affection except for bastards, lost souls, the tormented and Wandering Jews like myself. And the latter have never had for a country but an unobtainable dream or one lost early on.

A return that isn't a return, Yacine's death, this love abandoned on the paths of anguish and that then returns like a boomerang into impossibility . . . My Sultanas, antagonists, find themselves disjointed, dislocated. The Sultana of will has gone over there, her work in hand. Her desire washed out, she basks in the sun, withdrawn, a useless book in her hands. The other Sultana, here, lies in wait like a cat for some small pain or joy to sink her teeth into. But nothing ventures near her sharp claws. Passing time builds up and discharges elsewhere. It comes to her as a flat line; waiting for it gives way to lethargy. My two parts feed off of each other. Separated, they are both deactivated, defused. And I, who lived in their narrow junction, tumultuous and torn between . . . I find myself, in the name of their scission, drifting in a calm, detached from everything, frozen. Village of my birth, fatal pilgrimage.

Leaving the hospital, I stroll aimlessly. Not for very long. Very quickly, feverish eyes overcome my indifference, interrogate me, interrupt me. Crowd full of eyes, black wind, lightning and thunder. I stroll no longer. I cut through a crowd of eyes. I walk against eyes, between their fires. And yet I no longer have a body. I am nothing but tension losing my way between the past and the present, a haggard memory that recognizes no reference point in herself.

In the streets, the boys play soccer with anything: a punctured ball, a ball of rags, an empty sardine can . . . 'Madam! Madam! Madam! . . .' the same idiotic remarks, the same grotesque, simian gestures, the same showers of rocks stop their games, for a brief moment. Laughter, and they disarm and return to childhood. The little girls smile at me and blush. Like veritable little mothers, they bustle about very young children. The hooded women, cast in the role of foreigners, hurry toward I don't know what emergency. At the foot of the walls, the men bask in the sun. The men here are no longer but the remains of nomads, let loose in sedentary immobility, deprived of memory. Chickens cluck around them, search the ground, little steps, little pokes with their beaks. Dull-eyed sheep smell their dung. There isn't a single donkey. Why? Cars move forward by the repeated honking of their horns, drivers' tirades of imprecations cried out against the children blocking the street, exasperated spitting from the windows. Behind this neighborhood lie the ruins of the ksar, crumbling with memories.

All of a sudden, before me, the doorway of a house . . . I know this wooden henna-colored hand of Fatma above the door, this high staircase made of the same gray cement as the courtyard, and with a drainpipe pouring onto the street, I know these. The floor that one can guess is in the back, has a terrace, I know it. Low doorway, worn out by time, held firmly in place by two large barbaric façades in their stooped position faithfully waiting for me in the upheaval of present time. Since then, Fatma's hand has undoubtedly been dipped a thousand times in henna and a thousand times faded; the roughcast redone and undone according to wealth and the rare rains that fall here only to do more devastation. The emotion I feel again makes my body tremble and smothers me. I see this woman again. Her name was Emna. One fine day her husband decreed with an official paper in hand that henceforth her first name would be Sarah. She shrugged her shoulders. Israel, the French government, it was all so far away from her, much too far away from her desert. This foreign first name remained foreign to me. I kept Emna, for years my only source of tenderness. Her affection, which filled a little of the void left by the disappearance of my mother, had made me adopt the Jewish mellah. Emna would squeeze me against her breast, murmuring, 'My little bird, my little sparrow.' The convincing tenderness of this repetition, 'little, little,' gave back to me a bit of the childhood taken away by my mother. Large, very large breasts, a black dress, a brightly shining scarf, and her face, so beautiful with goodness; the welcoming crevice between her breasts where I would come and bury my eyes, my nose, my whole face. Curled up there, I breathed in her skin and recognized myself there; the shaded sand, the odor of amber. I no longer moved. She would laugh with tenderness. I would glance up with one eye and admire the smoothness of her cheeks, their ocher-brown color like the sand at sunset. Her eyes flooded me, their nocturnal velvety feel flowed onto the burns of my days. When she worked, I would stay near her. I wouldn't make any noise. I would watch her. In her home, the aroma of grilled peppers, the odors of basil, and Andalusian song intoxicated the morning. Because I straddled my own borders each day to go be with her, I gnawed at them, broke them, and transcended them. Her affection was the best antidote against the rejections I met, pieds-noirs, Jews, and Arabs, let loose in the village.[1] The joys of Independence were saddened by Emna's departure. With her I lost the last fragments of childhood. She made me an orphan for a second time. I want to sit down at this doorstep like we used to do together in the past. Emna, two distant letters, then Sarah the foreigner was en-

1. Pied-noir: literally 'black foot,' a name given to the French in Algeria.

gulfed by life; the silence of those who keep buried in themselves unbearable forevers.

Children around me and questions. Passersby stop and force me to turn around and go back. The jolts of my unconscious, at work in spite of my lethargy, have propelled me up to this point, up to this zone of love always lit inside of me. As a result, my second Sultana purrs, the honey of pain in her chest. Still, she'll spend days savoring it and getting over it.

Sundown's rosy light settles onto the village hum. Salmon and lilac colors in a sky finally too weary of wasting away. The palm grove is a knot of greenery on the dry wound of the wadi. All around the tops of the dunes, seat of aridity, the diabolical eye of eternity lying in wait. Here greenery has human fragility, shakiness, uncertainty hinted at in the crushing dogma of light.

Sitting on the terrace, across from the palm grove, I watch the sun go down. The ksar is on my right. I don't see it. A clump of palm trees separates me from it. I didn't go there, neither yesterday nor today. 'You don't want to go visit your house?' Salah said, endlessly surprised. No, I didn't want to! I haven't set foot there since my departure. And anyway, what can I be looking for there? The ruins of my memory long preceded those of the ksar . . . The latter only foreshadow for me their ghost. And anyway, ksour are precious only for their exoticism, for the rare tourists and for those who don't have to live there. As for me, I understand why their inhabitants sacrifice esthetics for a bit of convenience and roofs that don't melt into mud at the least rainfall. It's said that the ksar now shelters only goats, sheep, and the few donkeys that have still survived the invasion of cars. So what would I go do there? 'Why? Why?' That's how it is, period. 'Why' vulture, you'll have nothing from me that I don't want to deliver. I don't give a damn about the derogatory 'abnormal' that people can label me with.

Apart from this guy Chauvet, today at the hospital I saw only inpatients. What's that guy doing here? It's funny how he resembles Yacine from behind. The same build, the same hair. In the hospital, nothing very serious. The worrisome cases are evacuated to the city. And the hospital?

The water is cut off daily, there's a frequent lack of gloves, throwaway materials, disinfectants, dosed medications, the basics . . . I'll have to make do.

Examining this transplant patient in such a context was completely surreal. The beneficiary of a kind of medicine for the rich in the heart of the hospital of despair. Tomorrow morning I see patients. The two waiting rooms must be even more packed than before. At the end of the afternoon, I'll go to see little Dalila, this seed of all exiles.

Last night I slept to my heart's content in this hotel. That rested me. Maybe I'll stay there tomorrow. I'm preparing myself for this first night, alone, in that house. I simultaneously dread it and await it. During the day, I avoided this thought. But I felt it there, dense and secret, an impenetrable corner in the cavern of my mind. The sky grows dark. I go home and barricade myself in. I lock the door to Yacine's bedroom. I'll sleep on the couch. When I return to the living room, I find him sitting there. I open up my hand and, stunned, look at the bedroom key that I removed from the lock. His reproachful look confuses me. He shakes his head disapprovingly. He seems sick, and big circles create pockets under his eyes. I feel distraught. The venom of guilt twists my guts. Yacine gestures to me to sit on his knees. His call to me completely throws me off balance into a state of need, the desire for him. He doesn't say a word. His hands, his mouth deliciously pierce my skin. His eyes welcome my groans of pleasure with satisfaction. My sensual pleasure avenges him for my cowardice. The world reels in my head. I die in its collapse.

I feel so weary this morning. I hardly slept. I think I completely forgot to eat yesterday. I'm not even hungry. I dope myself up with black coffee that Khaled, the nurse, prepares for me. He adds a few drops of orange flower water and a touch of pepper to it. It's very good.

I become accustomed again to the metaphors of Algerian somatic language. The men come to me with a curious air extinguished by the mask of illness. They pull up chairs to my desk, collapse on them, breath out, make a face: 'Tabiba, I've got a door here that suddenly opened up.' They

[71]

show me chests or backs. 'It really, really hurts.' Or again, after some brief discomfort, their faces burdened: 'I have no more soul,' or 'My soul is dead,' to be translated as 'I've become impotent.' Their eyelids lowered, their lips suddenly paralyzed with shame, they would like to be able to immediately take back and swallow what they've just admitted. Too late. The infirmities or the amputations of the soul and the virulent dramas of existence crash on to my desk.

The women: 'My sister, something is giving me pain like knife stabs here and there, and also there, and here and here and here.' They show me their whole abdomen, their chest, shoulders, back, head, legs, arms . . . all at the same time. 'May Allah keep you from evil, when I get this, my head spins, I break out in a sweat, I vomit, my limbs feel smashed. And afterward I'm weak, I don't sleep, I don't eat, and all I want to do is stay in bed. Care for me please, my sister!' When everything is painful, in Algerian Arabic *koulchi*, it's a matter of the koulchite, a very widespread feminine pathology so well known here. The koulchite, symptomatic of feminine upheavals and distress.

I bandage wounds. I sew. I plaster. I examine and listen to long complaints. When I bend over my desk to write up a prescription, the women recover their eagle eyes and the sharpness of their beaks. They scrutinize me, size me up, dissect me, before daring: 'You have children?' The danger bell clangs in my head. If I answer in the negative, watch out for the avalanche of whys, the flashes of scandalized or sympathetic looks. I'll no longer be able to extricate myself. I evade the question with a learned: 'Here, I'm the one who asks questions, don't change roles!' Softened by a certain amount of laughter. Sighs of relief, smiles. I'm not totally a monster. In spite of my functions and my appearance, my body belongs to the league of candidates to the swollen body, to the faithful of the cult of the womb. They conclude: 'So you have children. How many? It's your mother who watches them? Are they doing well? May Allah protect them for you from the evil eye! And your husband, is he a doctor, too? Oh, my God, how complicated the world is now! By the way, where are you from? Tell me, my sister, where are you from?' As my only answer, I hand over my prescription. 'Excuse me, the other patients are waiting. Next!'

Three-thirty, finally no more patients.

'Come and eat at the house. My wife insists that you come.'

'No, thank you, Khaled. More than anything else, I need to rest quietly. Another time, I promise you.'

'Will you at least make something to eat for yourself? Halima, the cleaning woman who used to keep house for Yacine, often cooked for him without his even asking her.'

'We'll see about that later. Yes, yes, I cook for myself. Don't worry . . . If you need me at all tonight and I'm not at Yacine's, call me in town at the Sonatour Hotel. I'll stop by and see the in-patients again before going there. I'll leave my directions here on the table if anything new comes up. Don't hurry. Take the time to rest.'

'Okay, I'll see you tomorrow.'

I take off my smock. Yacine's is still hanging there. A silhouette without substance, a pale skin without a head, without arms, an enactment of waiting. I caress it, drop it, pick it up again, and put it on. It covers me all the way to my feet. I sniff the collar, plunge my hands into the pockets. In the right one, the contact with a piece of paper gives me a start. I grab it, unfold it. It's a white prescription, a nothingness prescription.

While leaving the hospital, I run into Ali Marbah, the Islamist tra-bendist—taxi driver. He must have been waiting for me, sitting on the low surrounding wall.

'You don't play around with me! I know who you are. I know you.'

Hearing these words, I feel a big release. I armor myself with disdainful calmness and walk past. His tics are exacerbated and they torture his face. With his shaggy beard and his wild-eyed expression, he really looks like an insane monkey. He yells at me from behind, 'I knew I'd already seen you! Why did you return to tempt and provoke us?'

'Are you a friend of Yacine's, too?' Dalila blurts out as soon as I reach her.

I came up to her slowly. I was so afraid she would flee at my approach. Perched on her dune, she observed my progress without moving at all.

[73]

'Yes.'

'You didn't come to see him.'

'No, because I live too far away, in France.'

'Do you have a little sister in Algeria?'

'No, she's . . .'

'She's with you in LaFrance?'

'No, I don't have a sister.'

'So she's dead . . . Yacine, he died of nothing. When it's nothing, it can be healed, can't it? Can you die of nothing even when you're a doctor?'

'You always die of something. We say "nothing" when we can't find the cause.'

'Is nothing a space that you don't see or don't know, a little like someone else's dream?'

'Nothing is neither a space nor a dream. Nothing is a word from nothingness. It takes away everything, even space.'

'Like death? It takes someone away from you, puts him in a rotting hole, and after, you have a hole in your life. Yacine, he doesn't come to my dreams. But I think of him a whole lot. But it's only tears that erase everything, even the other people from dreams. It makes me ghossa!'

'Ghossa, like you say, that's anger.'

'Yes, I know.'

'Who are these dream people?'

'You, you're his friend, will you be able to put Yacine in a book, like *The Bendir* and *The Little Sultan*?'

'*The Bendir* and *The Little Sultan*?'

Weary, she shrugs her shoulders and decides not to pay attention to my questions.

'Tell me about your school.'

'School? What d'you want to know about school? Ouarda says that school is no longer a space where you learn. She says that now it's a factory for morons and little Islamists. Little moronic Islamists like my brothers.'

'Yet you reflect and you question.'

[74]

'Yeah, but there aren't very many like me. I don't say that to put on airs, no. But since I'm the only girl in the house, it means that my parents don't bother me too much. And especially when I go out, they don't ever check for me at Ouarda's. They're afraid of making her mad. So I can come here and be left alone.'

'I understand you have a sister in France. So you're not an only daughter.'

'Well . . . yes. But she's never here. Fortunately there's Ouarda! Ouarda, she makes me read and learn. With her I really talk about things. She makes all my fears of threats that I get in school go away. She makes me think.'

'What are all these threats that the school inflicts on you?'

'These stupid things from the Hadith that want to make you live the way the prophet Muhammad's wives and daughters lived.[1] How many Muhammads have there been since that one? But if you refuse to follow this path, you're promised every kind of hell. The schoolmasters are so happy to tell you how they're going to boil you in a big vat of bad people. How they're going to have you torn in two by attaching you to two horses. How they'll . . .'

'Hmmm, I see. But you do read other things at school, don't you?'

'The reading at school is always the story of a good little girl who helps her mama while her brother plays outside. It's all I don't want to be, all I don't want to do.'

'I understand you!'

'Tell me first why the language we speak at home and in the street isn't school language?'

'Because the government, the people who've been ruling Algeria since Independence, have insisted it's a dialect.'

'My parents don't understand everything on the radio and TV. You always have to explain to them. And us young people, we speak one lan-

1. Hadith: the prophet Muhammad's words and his answers to material and spiritual questions.

guage with the schoolmasters and schoolmistresses, another at recess and in the street.'

'That's the real problem.'

'But why? Why'd they do that?'

'When Independence came, the rulers decreed that two of the Algerian languages, North African Arabic and Berber, were unworthy of official business. Yet their centuries-long resistance to different invasions is proof of their life and should have made them sacred. Alas! As for the third language of the country, French, it became the language of those who sold out, the 'colonial henchmen.' You see, it's an efficient way to push aside some and discredit others, those who could protest against the regime; a tactic to silence everyone. In the end, they managed to.'

'So they said our language is nothing. And now the Islamists say we don't even know our religion. We're just a bunch of failures, ever since our grandfathers, the grandfathers of our grandfathers.'

'Yes, in a way. The people, they mutilated it and abandoned . . .'

'You know, the first time I went to school, my mom had put a necklace and a bracelet made of morjane on me, that were her mom's.

'In French you say "coral." '

'Coral, yes, I know. I was so happy to have on my grandmother's jewelry and also because I thought my teacher was going to teach me all sorts of beautiful things. You know what she said as soon as she saw me? "Go on, take off that necklace and bracelet! Give them to me! And I want to see you with long sleeves this afternoon!" I didn't put on a dress with long sleeves. She never gave me back my grandmother's necklace and bracelet. That made my mom cry. I asked the teacher for them several times. She turned all red. Once she slapped both my cheeks for that. And then all she taught me was forbidden things. So in class, I plugged my head and hated her in silence.'

'Your mom didn't go demand them back from her?'

'No, she's too afraid of people who are so important . . . why is Arabic just the language of fear, of shame and sins, especially when you're a girl?'

'A language is only what's made of it! In other times, Arabic was the language of knowledge and poetry. It still is for a few handfuls of rebels or of the privileged classes. You have to continue to resist and to take from elsewhere what you don't find at school.'

A great sense of sadness comes over her face. Her eyes wander and come to rest in the faraway regions of the sand, then come back and land on me.

'Do you have brothers?'

'No, I've never had any.'

'My mom and people say that brothers are good. They say that they protect you, that they're a barrier against h'chouma.'

'Against shame.'

'Yes, against shame. You, you do like the roumi, you correct the Algerian words. Yacine, he doesn't do that. He's used to it. Us real Algerians, we're always mixing words.'

'Because I'm not a real Algerian?'

'No. Us, the real ones, we mix French with Algerian words. You, you're a real mix, so you don't mix words anymore. When you study over there, you become a real mix. Don't get mad, okay? Now here, it's not shameful anymore to be a migrant. The zoufris migrants, they don't study.[1] So even over there, they don't become mixed. They just mix words, even more than us. But that doesn't matter, the women from here all want to marry their daughters to them. They say: "They have money, and my daughter'll live in LaFrance, and then I'll go on "facation" over there." '

'You know, "real mix" suits me fine. And you, do you think there's no mix at all in you?'

'I say, "we real ones," but I don't know if I'm real. My mother says that us and a lot of people from the desert, grandfathers, grandfathers of our grandfathers . . .'

'You say "our forefathers." '

'She says our forefathers were all blacks who came from the other side

---

1. *Zoufris:* workers.

[77]

of the desert. Yacine, he says that the grandfather, no, his forefathers, they were maybe Jews, that a lot of Kabyle are like that. Do you think there are people who are real sons of real people?'

'I think a mix is the only truth. All the rest is only hypocrisy or ignorance.'

'When I think about all that, it mixes up my head and I don't know anything anymore.'

'It's not very serious. You've got all of your life ahead of you to ponder the question. A minute ago, what did you want to tell me about brothers?'

'I think it's good not to have brothers. Brothers just bother you, that's all. Are brothers in LaFrance so stupid and mean?'

'A lot less so, because they have no authority over their sisters.'

'Me, I don't have a sister at home and I have seven brothers. If I listen to them, all I'll do is obey and work seven times over, all the time. I don't. I escape in the dunes or at Ouarda's and seven times over I hate them in my head. Do you study in LaFrance?'

'I finished my studies several years ago. I work.'

'What kind of work?'

'I'm a doctor.'

'Like Yacine.'

'Yes. Yacine and I did part of our studies together.'

'And your father?'

'I don't have one.'

'That's why you don't give a damn, you can leave and come back when you want. There isn't anyone who wants to marry you off bessif and prevent you from studying and walking and finding the space you want.[1] Maybe all fathers and all boys have to be dead so that girls can return.'

Her enlarged eyes stare at me without blinking, without seeing me. For a few moments she remains tense, completely involved in her pondering, in her internal conflicts.

'Is it since your sister no longer comes that you've had such thoughts?'

'It's been since I was very little, since I know that I can't turn off all of

1. *Bessif:* forcefully.

the earth's light, or make things and people disappear just by closing my eyes.'

'What do you mean?'

'When I was little and I would close my eyes, I thought I was erasing the whole world. When my brothers were angry at me, I would say to them, "Shut up, leave me alone, otherwise I'll turn you off." I'd close my eyes, I wouldn't see them anymore, then I believed they didn't exist anymore. But now I know that it's not true. So I leave the house.'

I look at her and wonder whether at her age I felt this candid rage, this stubborn vehemence. Certainly, but much less clearly.

'If my sister, Samia, marries a roumi, what will her children be like?'

'Her children will be even more real mixes than me.'

'Yes, but what will her children, Samia's children be like?'

'Well, that'll depend on the man she'll marry.'

'Will they be named Muhammad and Ali and Aïcha, or what? Will they be blond or red-headed or brown mixed with black like me?'

'It depends.'

'I don't like "it depends." You can say some "maybes" if you like. There's space in "maybe." "It depends" is hard and twisted. Like the stonemason Laouedj's walls.[1] He forgets the plumb wire in his pocket and makes zigzags on the walls.'

Her serious manner and her furor enchant me.

'I don't know your sister. If she were to marry a Frenchman, her children could have Arabic first names, yes. Physically, they'd resemble a bit of their father, their mother, or their grandparents. That's why I said "it depends."'

She calms down.

'A French father, can he have a boy named Muhammad and a girl named Fatima?'

'If he wants to, of course.'

My answer floors her. She's able to smile again.

---

1. Laouedj: the Twisted One.

'The French are better than us. Because here, nobody can call their son Jean or their daughter Marie . . . and you, what about your daughter?'

'I don't have one.'

'But when you have one.'

'I won't. That's the only thing I'm sure about. But maybe one day I'll adopt a child.'

'I think my sister, Samia, is like you. She won't have a child because of everything that . . .'

She loses herself in thought. I ask: 'Do you talk with your mother? For example, do you tell her what you just told me?'

A vigorous no with her head.

'My mother, I don't tell her anything. Sometimes she also gets my brothers angry with her. But if I say anything against them, she hits me. She says I have to obey them. Yet she defends me. Once I told her about the people in my dreams. She was worried for several days. She thought I was crazy or struck down by the evil eye or a djinn. She wanted to take me to the m'rabet.[1] Now I don't say anything more to her. Ouarda, the schoolteach – no, the professor – says it's better I don't worry her too much. She says I'm already a worry for her, because I'm a girl. She says to us girls that we're just worries full of worries! It's not much fun!'

She turns toward the expanse of the erg and continues.

'No, it isn't very much fun to be a girl. Your mother, you only tell her lies or you keep quiet. Fortunately, she,' she designates the dunes, 'always comes to see me each time I'm here. I tell her everything, even what I hide from Ouarda and Yacine. She listens to me. She never gets mad.'

'Who is "she?"'

She doesn't answer. Her eyes sweep across the dunes and touch lightly on the palm trees before returning to me.

'Before you came here, were trees red in LaFrance?'

'Some, yes, like each autumn.'

---

1. M'rabet (or marabout): in North Africa, a saintly person whose grave is worshiped.

[80]

'I'd really like to see a red tree. Samia says that each time the dates are ripe here, the trees are red in LaFrance.'

'Yes, it's true.'

'A red palm tree would be pretty. Here, the sky, the sand, and the palm trees are always the same color, and there aren't any trees.'

'And palm trees?'

'The palm tree reaches for the sky, closed. I'd really like big trees that open up and make a lot of shade and become red when the dates are ripe and that are all bare, just made of wood, when it's cold, and that make baby leaves, all clean, when it's springtime. Is springtime pretty too?'

'Yes, very. You'll see the seasons in northern Algeria.'

'I've never seen the Tell. I've never seen the ocean. I've never seen big trees that open up. I've never seen spring. Samia says that spring in the desert is only sand wind. She says that people from here can't change because each year the sand wind buries them, while others are experiencing a new spring. She says that men can't like women and girls where there are never spring flowers. She says life is like a feast with red trees. What's a feast?'

'A celebration meal.'

'I don't like celebrations. They always make me want to cry. But about this, my sister, Samia, exaggerates; the sand wind is very beautiful, very strong, stronger than all the other winds. It changes the sky, it erases it. And anyway, here there are also men who love women and girls, like Yacine, except there aren't very many.'

'So haven't you ever left Tammar?'

'Us, we never leave, and nomads are like my sister, Samia, they've lost their space. So they don't come anymore to the wadi. Sometimes in my dreams, the palm trees are red and there's lots of pretty clouds in the sky: white ones, clear gray and dark gray ones, a lot of violet-colored and even black ones. They make shadows on the whole earth. There's water sleeping in the wadi. A transparent dream. You can see its outside and its inside. You see brilliant pebbles, like wet stars, at the bottom, you also see clouds that dance in the water and palm trees dancing lying down. There's grass and flowers and butterflies. There's nomad khéïma and their camels.[1] There's lots of grandmothers telling about voyages. The Little Sultan is swimming in the wadi and is watching his star. The Bendir is playing his tin drum and is breaking apart bunches of dates. The children run to eat the dates and cry out with joy. Djaha is having fun. He has a gandoura the color of a white cloud. His donkey has blue eyes and a pink ribbon around his neck. Targou is up to her tricks just to make the women laugh. And the women don't say anything mean around her. They're not afraid of her, no. They're laughing together. I go from my hiding place to the top of a palm tree. When I don't want to see anybody, I climb up there. A red palm tree must be beautiful.'

'Yes, certainly.'

'Look, there are some men over there who are eyeballing us.'

'Who are looking at us.'

'Samia says that. She says, here people don't look. They eyeball. They've got their eyes glued to your skin, glued to you all the way through to your blood, like bloodsuckers, like grasshoppers, everywhere on you, even under your clothes and even, it makes lumps in your chest. It makes you mix up your feet so you fall.'

'Stumble.'

'Yes, stumble. She says that with everything that's forbidden by the desert, by Allah, by your mother's customs, all that is hungered for, all that is thirsted for, your eyes have concentrated misery, all of hell in their pupil. She says that because of this hell, eyes are burning and burned. They can't look. All they can do is eyeball. They have to touch, palpate, pinch things like blind people do with their hands, just to know what it is. I think Samia, my sister, is right. That's why I eyeball my dreams so strongly. My eyes touch them. So I think they exist for real. What's real?'

'Whatever one feels very strongly is real.'

---

1. *Khéïma:* tents.

She ponders and then decides, 'I have to go home.'

She gets up and stays there, obviously with no great desire to leave.

'Eyeball him, the guy coming from over there. His name is Vincent, like a m'rabet where he's from, but him, he's not cherif.[1] From a distance, he looks like Yacine. Vincent is maybe a real son of real people, isn't he?'

1. *Cherif*: descended from the prophet Muhammad.

6

VINCENT

I'm waiting for her, and in the grip of this waiting, I no longer know what to do with either my body or my time.

After breakfast and a walk in the palm grove, I go back to my room. I take out the radio–cassette player that had remained in my suitcase. I put on Beethoven's Ninth and I settle down in front of the glass door facing the dunes. Like the tide, the symphony rises within me, glorious, overwhelming, and in the explosion of choirs above the brilliant instruments, I'm carried on its wave to the wild call of the erg. Its waves lick the dunes, roll over them and whisper to them of other shores, other faces, of alluring forests buried in secret lichen, of burning dreams in the white heart of northern winters crackling with cold. Here, this hymn becomes a celebration of the sky, an exultation of the light that fills my wait with fervor and joy.

Moh came to see me at the end of the morning, and I had all kinds of trouble getting rid of him without ruffling his sensibilities too much. In fact, in order to succeed, I had to promise him that I'd go eat at his place the next day at noon.

'And what are you going to do all afternoon and evening?'

'Believe it or not, I have to work,' I lied.

'Work?'

'Yes, I have something to write up . . . a document to finish that I've let drag for a long time. It's partly for that reason that I came here to seek some peace and quiet.'

'You come to the desert to work,' he grumbled, not very convinced.

I stayed there, one hand on my kidney, between Rilke and Beethoven, between the dunes and the sky, patiently waiting. One falls in love again, as one falls into childhood, with a memory and a conscience cleansed of their now cumbersome and obsolete defenses.

Dalila has been perched on her dune for a little while already, and I've had to force myself not to join her, when Sultana arrives. I see her park the strange pink car in front of the hotel, go in and come out just as fast, and walk toward the dune. My heart speeds up and pounds against my ribs as if it wanted to escape from me and rush toward her. She's wearing a periwinkle blue dress. A long white scarf floats along the length of her body. She has a big white handbag and shoes of the same color that she removes and holds in her hand when she tackles the sand. Her jet black curls fall like a mane onto her shoulders.

I go downstairs to the lounge and wait there, ready, but I want to leave them alone for a moment. I spy on them from the lounge window as I try to calm my crazy heart.

The discussion starts up and soon becomes animated, because Dalila uses lively gestures with which she punctuates her anger and her convictions. Like a cat, I lie in wait for them, like a cat who tastes and measures the succulent slowness of time, in the same tempo as its voluptuous purr.

When Dalila finally gets up, I quickly leave the hotel so I won't miss her and so as not to give the other one the time to slip away. I've just reached them when the call of the muezzin rips the sunset. Dalila is startled.

'It's late. I'm going to get scolded. I have some things to ask you,' she adds, addressing me in particular. 'You aren't going to leave?'

'No, no, I'm not leaving yet.'

Cooing laughter. She slowly leaves.

'Why are you staying here?' the woman asks abruptly, and without waiting for my answer: 'Look at them, it's impossible to have any peace even for an instant.'

A group of men standing in front of the hotel will not release us from their gaze. They don't seem friendly.

'I imagine that must be very tiresome . . .'

'Here, "tiresome" is a euphemism. Pushed to an extreme, however, even the tragic becomes caricature, something burlesque, something grotesque. But let them look their fill, let them eyeball us, as Dalila says, let them condemn, vociferate, or insult, they'll never be able to reach the emptiness in me.'

'The emptiness?'

'Yes, where there's no longer anyone, this "lost space," Dalila would say . . . How do you experience someone else's organ in your body?' she asks me point-blank.

'Like . . . someone similar and different, bound to me. I'll never be able to consider that I have of this other person only an organ, to conceive of a human as being made of spare parts from the transplant bazaar. This kidney is only our meeting point.'

'It's funny,' she says with a little nervous laugh. 'You integrate a missing person. I break up. I'm absent from myself. But is there a difference between you and me? Between the absence in one's self and the absence of one's self? I don't know. I don't know.'

'Because you feel broken up?'

'Yes, into several dispersed me's.'

'But why this feeling?'

'Maybe because of the constant presence of something unacceptable and because of something broken inside of me. You lose your cohesion. You become several beings that can't be grasped, like exaggerated metaphors of yourself, projected into what is possible, what is tolerable. But being so scattered doesn't mean that you no longer exist, doesn't it?'

'On the contrary, it means being in absolute liberty, outside of your body, outside of time, and outside of their contingencies. I would have

[86]

liked to have felt that. As for me, for years I could only be in a sick self, held captive in a body that had become anemic and traitorous. You doctors, even being in daily contact with dialysis patients, you can only have an intellectual approach to what they feel. You stay on the outside as active observers. The patient endures. He is trapped in an inferior state. In a state of danger that he cannot master.

'You create a "vascular opening." You "arterialize" a vein to give it a sufficient rate of flow for circulation outside the body. You call that an "arterial-venous" bridge, a "fistula." For me, the sick person, this thing was a little heart beating at my wrist, an electric relay that plugged me into an intelligent mechanical apparatus, that took me into a horrible world. But that horror had become an absolute necessity for me. My skin was covered with scars and abnormalities, with holes made of odds and ends, accessible or plugged up. It no longer defined a totality. And watching my blood leaping about in tubes, my eyes would go liquid. They became like inquisitive isotopes. Artery of the artificial kidney, its fiber filters, its vein, they returned to my body carrying the blood. They flowed, ran in this state of danger. On alert, they dampened secretions, looked for tumors. Fear surreptitiously grabbed hold of me and turned me onto myself like a cuttlefish. I drowned in the depths of my fear, in the ink of sickness. But you, why this flight into dispersal?'

'I don't know. In part, without a doubt, because of the dead child in me. Maybe also because of the lands. The desert. Oran. Paris. Montpellier. A division of lands and a division of my interior countryside. Land that is dear to you, and that you're forced to leave, keeps you forever. By leaving, you become unused to yourself, you no longer live in yourself. You're nothing but a stranger everywhere. An impossible halt and an even more impossible return.'

'Did you say a dead child?'

'Yes, the child that I once was and who holds a grudge against the adult for having survived her. The adult disowned it. She repudiated it. She disinherited her and cut her into pieces. Having stayed in her ksar, she's wandering there, brushing up against the walls with the light in her eyes

[87]

gone, on endless ruminations, unable to forget. She never ceases to persecute the one who lived, however. She keeps her in check and holds her
completely. She is her first exile.'

'There you are looking very somber . . . and who are you with this diversity? Or should I perhaps say adversity?'

'Adversity, yes. Who am I, with such a situation? I don't know very well.
It's an indescribable sensation. Who was it who said that the fear of insanity was already insanity? Fernando Pessoa, I think. Maybe I'm sort of
at that point. From which comes the flight into several intertwined beings.'

She lifts her eyes and suddenly stares at me with embarrassment.

'I've never spoken so much about it before . . . I don't know why I'm
burdening you so much.'

She crouches down as if getting ready to leave. I'll do anything to keep
her here.

'Oh! On the contrary, you're not burdening me,' I cry out eagerly. 'For
a long time I haven't said anything to others either. I've learned at my ex-
pense that from the moment a terrible discrimination lands on you, not
only are you no longer the same person, but the whole world has changed
on you. Imagine . . . Imagine that you wake up one day just like the others, or so you think. You look at yourself in the mirror: same face burdened by sleep. The same old circles that no longer surprise you. The
same eyes that observe themselves with the same boredom. You go to the
bathroom. You know that you can't do anything before you've emptied
the bladder that weighs you down each morning. Oh, shit! You pee out
blood! Without your knowing it, something is there, it has settled into
you and is gnawing on you. It abruptly reveals itself to you by this bloody
interruption of habit. You stay perplexed in front of the toilet bowl full of
red, unable to flush. You reflect for a moment. You realize it's your kidney.
I have to have a plan! For most mortals, what can be the matter with a
kidney that's pissing blood? Apparently, many do this, forming mineral
deposits like old teakettles, it's well known, it's commonplace. That's re-
assuring. You remember that one of your friends had suffered terribly

from this. You poke your stomach and you're almost disappointed to feel nothing. "This mustn't be a very bad kidney stone," you conclude. You flush and your blood leaves like excrement into the sewers.'

Once again she'd let herself drop onto the sand. She looks toward the expanse of the erg, but I know she's listening to me. I continue.

'From doctors to lab tests, you end up in a nephrology department. There they don't ask you if you know anything. They deal out everything to you. "Nephrology, from the Greek *nephros*, kidney," a mouth informs you from the height of its importance. They exclude your little reckonings. And with a barbaric word they nail you with your real problem. "What's that?" you say, stunned. They answer you with a definitive adjective: "Incurable!" "Incurable? Incurable?" This word scrapes your mouth. You don't find a single drop of saliva to swallow it with. You've been dried out. Incurable!

'Surrounding you are other "patients" with other labels and at various stages of their inability to be cured. A catastrophic scenario of your immediate future. Yes, immediate future, because besides "incurable," the only words concerning you, from the medical jargon, that you have remembered are "rapidly progressive evolution." You leave stunned.

'The first time you leave the hospital, a profound metamorphosis occurs in you. By means of a paradoxical effect from the shock you've just received, the short-sightedness with which you have until now approached the world has disappeared. And this brutally readjusted, sharpened vision becomes your second illness. For the first time you discover life as you have never seen it, with its cruel features and all of eternity concentrated into an instant. You become gifted with a sort of cosmic acuteness for probing the exterior and the interior microscopic worlds.'

'Yes, I understand.'

'Then, consultation upon consultation, the worsening of your condition and the avalanche of warnings and medical interdictions: be careful of the hyper-thingamajig! Watch out for the hypo-thing! So many warnings and rebellions lying in wait for you: potassium, calcium, phosphorus, salt, water . . . You're nothing but that. You're no longer anything but

[89]

a bit of disorderly chemistry with a skull and crossbones at its two extremities: hyper and hypo, a fear that dances the jig between the hyper of stress and the hypo of depression. Nephrology is a hyper-medicine that has built itself by saving individuals from death, certainly, but by making of them, in the same stroke, hypo-men serving an octopus machine with tubular tentacles: the artificial kidney. It's that or death! Circulate, there's no choice.'

'Were you on dialysis for a long time?'

'Five years. Five years during which I tried to save myself from the morbid effects of chronicity, to tear a little of my dignity away from a despotic and voracious medical apparatus. I dialyzed myself alone at home at night so I could keep on working during the day. The result: my girlfriend got the hell out, my circle of friends drooped like a suddenly wilted flower. But the worst is to live with this seed of death in one's body.'

'What do you mean?'

'Two of your organs have refused to quietly do their work in order to die, thereby setting in motion the process, and postponing it just a little, of your complete death without the machine's intervention. You're immediately suspicious of your other organs. What are *they* plotting against me too? The lack of any sign from them is nothing but a sly menace. Aren't they all conspiring against me? "And my liver, doctor? And my heart, doctor? And my stomach?" He reassures you. "Everything else is fine." Fine? Except that all the rest suffers from kidney failure and even your pecker is nothing more than a piece of lifeless meat. No wee-wee and no hard-on.'

'But now, with this exceptional transplant, the nightmare is over with, isn't it?'

'Yes, over with. Now what eats at me is this absence transplanted into me, a question that will never have an answer. One day the telephone rings. You lift up the receiver: "Mister Chauvet, we have a kidney for you!" This moment, at once anticipated and feared, knocks you off your feet.

You'd have so much liked to have had someone near you at this moment. You're alone. You've been alone for so long that it's become your normal state. No one to kiss. No one to take refuge with. But in a city hospital, a piece of dead flesh calls you and waits for you in a cold receptacle. You will never be alone again. A dead kidney that is placed next to one of your own dead kidneys. A dead kidney that they join up to the artery, to the vein and the ureter of your dead kidney. A dead kidney that lives again from your blood, that gives you this simple and until now unsuspected joy: the ability to piss again. A handful of cells from another body liberates you from the machine's prison.'

'Do you know whose kidney this is?'

'It's a woman's, an Algerian woman's.'

'An Algerian woman's!'

'Yes, at least in origin. I know nothing else about her. What a feeling to know that I had the same tissue identity as a woman and, moreover, a woman from elsewhere! Those who tell lies about the races would do well to take a glance at genetics!'

There you have it. I threw myself, my anxieties and torments, my wee-wee depression, my inner organs' suicide, my feeling of mutilation, my solitary past and present salutary state of being a twin, its strange solidarity, jumbled all together at her feet so she wouldn't leave. I almost threw in, to top it off, the memory of my mother, anti-Semitism, the camps, and the whole upheaval. I held back. There remained some modesty, despite my passion. But her eyes are so far-off, so inaccessible. The men who still keep watching us are starting to worry me but don't bother her. Where is she? Now who is she? A little girl who died from I don't know what in Aïn Nekhla and who wanders in her death? A woman passing through Paris in a state of anonymity who, in exile, has no borders? A woman walking along a French beach whose eyes take in the Mediterranean, this immense heart beating between the two shores of her sensitivity?

'What do you do?'

That's completely like her, that way of catching you off guard, impromptu, with a question. Certainly a gift of her diversity. While one of her, out on a jaunt, makes sure you lose your way, her other self comes and surprises you from behind.

'I'm a math professor at the University of Paris.'

'But we're not on break as far as I know.'

'That's right. After the transplant, I took a sabbatical year to travel and erase the hardships I suffered because of my illness.'

'You're not going to stay here for your entire sabbatical year, are you?'

'No. After the desert, I'll go bask in the sun in a sailboat on the shores of the Mediterranean.'

'In a sailboat?'

'Yes. I arrived in Oran by sailboat.'

'In the middle of the ocean, you must feel the same sensations as in the desert, don't you?'

'Yes, completely. Next spring I'll sail toward Greece and Turkey. If that tempts you, you would be welcome to come along.'

'It's getting late!'

She's right, the sunset is no longer on fire. As if contagious, a muted night reaches the sky. A brown shadow is already dozing in the troughs of the dunes. With their fronds the palm trees trap the sky and condense it in their trunks.

'I'm thirsty,' she says as she gets up. We go down the dune slowly.

Passing in front of the men squatting beside the hotel stirs up a thick cloud of muttering. I feel ill at ease.

'Sometimes it's an advantage not to understand the language of a country,' she hurls at me sharply.

'I did understand the displeasure, anyway.'

In the hotel bar a few men are seated in front of their beers. She goes toward the counter and orders one, too. The waiter serves it to her with unconcealed rage.

With a half smile and addressing my reflected image in the mirror: 'Do you know that in most big cities, bistros refused to serve women? Elsewhere, the problem didn't even arise. In spite of everything, there's some progress,' she says ironically, loud enough to be heard by the whole room.

An abrupt silence falls on the men. To break it, I order a pastis.[1] And I blush as I notice my voice trembling. The waiter shrugs his shoulders and exclaims, 'Pastis, pastis! All out! There's only beer and only sometimes. Pastis is in Marseilles. Here, before, there was anisette. You know what anisette is? But anisette left with the pieds-noirs. The pieds-noirs, they knew how to live. Eh? You have to tell the truth, or *Allah*!' he says, addressing his audience. Then he starts up again for my benefit.

'Ouach?[2] Girls, are they hatta in France?'[3]

A forced laugh echoes in him. Evidently, his jest has slackened the tension by a notch.

'What does "hatta" mean?' I ask the young woman.

' "Hatta" means "zazou," the in thing to do, as you say in France,' replies the waiter.

'So give me a beer, please.'

In an abrupt voice, while serving me, he asks the young woman a question in Arabic. She ignores him and continues to stare at the mirror with a vague look on her face. Once again the silence weighs heavily. In the mirror, the men's eyes pierce like arrows.

'Do you have a cigarette? I left my pack in my office.'

I hand her one, feeling more and more uncomfortable. 'What does he want to know?'

'Who I am.' Then scornfully looking the waiter up and down: 'We're certainly not from the same country!' Then grabbing her purse, she takes some change out of it, which she leaves on the counter.

---

1. Pastis: a popular alcoholic drink flavored with anise.

2. *Ouach:* 'Well?' 'So?' A word specific to the region of Oran.

3. *Hatta:* cool, hip, swinging.

'I'll do it, I'm paying!'

'Good-bye.'

I abandon my beer and dash after her. 'Why are you leaving so quickly? And I wanted to invite you for dinner.'

'I can't stay here. And anyway, being seen with you will cause you problems. Besides, someone's waiting for me.'

'Your patients, yes, I understand.'

She continues toward the car without saying anything.

'Can I call you if I need you?'

She opens the door, dives into the car, opens her bag, digs around in it, pulls out a piece of paper and a pen, scribbles two telephone numbers.

'Here, the number at Yacine's house and the hospital's. Good-bye.'

She speeds away. I'm unhappy about it. After a moment spent feeling distracted, I return to the bar. My beer is warm and tastes like piss.

'Who the hell is that woman?'

'A doctor.'

'A doctor? Even if she's a doctor, a woman isn't going to drink beer and speak like that to men in a bar!'

I leave the place. I walk in the street, in my state of confusion. I walk for a long time. The night is good for me. I'm not dragging a Moh or a trail of children behind me. I can wander about aimlessly, think freely. This evening, the first coolness, my first shiver. It does me good. It's late when I finally stop in front of a cheap restaurant.

'Can I get something to eat?'

'Batata koucha,' a fat old man who seems nice announces to me.

'What's that?'

'Hey, potatoes baked in the oven!' he proclaims as if it were obvious.

The oven-baked potatoes are prepared in a stew. It doesn't matter, they're really delicious.

'Do you want a little wine?'

'Do you have any?'

'Hey, Tayeb's got everything!'

A wink of the eye and he disappears behind a curtain.

'Give that a taste for me and we'll talk later. I'm the one who bottled it and everything! You'll see, it's good.'

'I'm tasting it.'

His eye sparkles, his mustache trembles.

'Hmmm, great, great!'

'Great, huh? My pal in El Malah, ex–Rio Saldo, he takes a good vine and he makes his wine à la pied-noir, not à la "moro." You know this expression from around here?'

'Which one?'

'Trabajo moro, poco y malo!'[1] He bursts out laughing.

'What d'you want, you gotta laugh at yourself a little; if you don't, you croak from sadness. Allah is great! Ow, ow, the wine we used to have! Me, I go fetch it over there in quantity and I bottle it, only for connoisseurs. The others, they drink anything, even an Islamic poison: half oil, half Mafia, half balls. What d'you want? That's how our country is today, maaleich.[2] Allah is great.'

He sits down in front of me, scratches the back of his head, and pushes his chechia toward the front.

'I'll give you a round,' I propose.

'Only to please you,' he affirms, in an easygoing manner.

He gets up and bounces off to fetch a glass. I serve him.

'How come there's no one here?'

'Hey, you can be informal with me! The local men can't eat out, only the ones passing through. There's only you tonight. The guys from here, they just come here to drink before they go home or after eating, it depends. Sometimes I keep my batata koucha for three days, carefully, in the fridge, and later I give it to the street children. What d'you want? That's how it is. Even in the desert we don't have tourists, and the ones who do come, they bring their food with them. What d'you want? Allah is great.'

---

1. *Trabajo moro, poco y malo!*: 'Arab work, little and badly done,' a Spanish aphorism quoted by the French.

2. *Maaleich:* It doesn't matter. Too bad.

[95]

'You have kids?'

'I have two grown girls at the university. They do well. I say to my girls, stay in the big city, even if it's hard, at least nobody there knows you. And here, it's not a life. If you fart sideways, even dead people know. They know what noise you made and even the smell! So when I want to see my girls I take their mother and I go to Oran. And I also have four boys in high school. What d'you want? Allah is great.'

He takes out a tobacco pouch with a 'shit' compartment.[1] He rolls himself a cigarette, copiously moistens it with his tongue, and hands it to me.

'You want it?'

'I've never smoked any.'

'Oh, try!'

I take the cigarette from his hand and smoke while I'm drinking. A sort of euphoric torpor overtakes me. For me, Tayeb's talk is juicy. His joviality, his conviviality, his simplicity, everything about him delights me. A good-natured face, serene, perhaps the true face of Algeria. I leave him when his cheap restaurant is full. He rolls me a last cigarette, 'for the road.' I promise to return.

I find the hotel deserted. Once in my room, I want to call her in Aïn Nekhla. In vain I try to reason with myself, looking at my watch, whose hands point to midnight. As I turn about in the cramped space of the room, like others turn their tongues seven times in their mouth before speaking, my need to hear her is irrepressible.

I dial the 'number of Yacine's house.' Someone answers immediately.

'Hello, pardon me for calling so late, I wanted to talk with you so much.'

She doesn't answer.

What nerve!

'If I'm bothering you, tell me so.'

Again, no answer.

1. Shit: hashish.

[96]

'All evening I've only been thinking about you. It'd be great if you came with me on the boat.'

She remains silent.

'I think I'm bothering you so late.'

She persists in her silence.

'Excuse me. Good night.'

'Wait!' she cries out.

'Yes?'

'Wait . . . A car followed me all the way from Tammar to Aïn Nekhla.'

'You should be careful. A woman alone driving at night on a deserted road, that can be dangerous!'

'They didn't attack me. They just followed me.'

'Do you have any idea who it was?'

'There was no one in the car.'

'What do you mean? A car follows you on the road and you affirm that it was empty?'

'Yes. It stayed constantly at about fifty meters behind me. At one point I stopped . . .'

'You're foolish!'

'It also stopped. That's when I became suspicious. I put the car in reverse. The other didn't move. I moved a little closer. In spite of the blinding brightness of the headlights, I could clearly see that there was nobody in the car.'

'The driver must have ducked down.'

'I think there was no one in that car.'

'There wasn't?'

'That's right. When I arrived here, it stopped right after me. It's still there, the motor on, headlights on and aimed at the house. There's nobody in the car.'

'Why don't you call the police?'

'Why do you want me to call the police? To meet with the same skepticism as yours? No, thank you!'

'Aren't you afraid?'

'Yes, a little, and especially because Yacine refuses to even look at me tonight.'

'Your friend Yacine?'

'Yes.'

'But he's dead!'

'Yes . . . but he's there in front of his easel. He's painting and he's ignoring me.'

'What's he painting?'

'A woman from behind.'

'I think you're too tired. Your nerves must be a bit frayed. Was Yacine very dear to you?'

'Yes. But I broke up with him and left. A long time ago. Sometimes you have to leave even those people you love.'

'Do you want me to come over?'

'No. Why doesn't he want to look at me? That's intolerable to me!'

'But he's dead, for goodness' sake! You should chase away all of these visions, go to bed, and try to sleep.'

'I won't be able to.'

'Then I'm coming over. I want to be near you so much. I want to see this car that rolls along empty and also this dead man who gets up to paint.'

I hang up without leaving her the time to say no again.

Not a living soul to be seen on the highway and in the streets of Aïn Nekhla. The night is dark, but I have no trouble finding Yacine's house, some hundred meters from the hospital. A big white building. A mix of colonial and Moorish architectural styles. Only the pink car is parked in front. Light filters through the shutters.

I climb up the front steps. I ring the doorbell. She opens for me. Her eyes seem enormous, frozen and deserted. She lets me in without a word, without showing either annoyance or pleasure. I step inside. In the middle of the living room, there's an easel with an empty canvas. I turn toward her.

'He left when you rang the doorbell. He took the painting he was working on with him. The car also left as soon as the noise from yours was audible.'

'You're destroying yourself!'

She shrugs her shoulders.

'You're not going to start in too, are you?'

'Start in on what?'

'Start lecturing me. Start suspecting me.'

'Who else is lecturing you?'

'My nurse, Khaled, and Salah.'

Her lost look, her absent eyes are painful to see.

'Have you had dinner?'

'I wasn't hungry.'

'Do you want me to prepare something for you to eat now?'

'Do I look sick enough to create so much concern?'

'You look exhausted.'

I go toward her. I take her in my arms. She doesn't resist. I carry her like a child to the end of the hallway. I open the first door. I lay her on the bed. She closes her eyes. I kneel down next to her. I caress her face, the curls of her hair. I kiss her. She puts her arms around me. I'm out of my depth. When our climax reaches its highest point, she says with a sigh, 'Yacine.'

7

SULTANA

I get up feeling dizzy and wanting to vomit. My stomach contracts in vain. Not even a bit of liquid to bring up. Just this piercing pain. I lie down on the bathroom floor. The backward surge of blood digs into my head, buzzes in my deafened ears. Then little by little, everything blurs. I get up carefully. I splash my face with cold water, then drink a few sips, and feel them descending the length of an endless intestine and getting lost in foreign rumblings. I make some coffee and force myself to eat a cracker.

As I leave the house to go to the hospital, the street seems surprisingly empty to me. I'm getting ready to cross when a loud screeching of tires startles me. Two steps away from me, Ali Marbah slams on his brakes like a maniac.

'There's no point in making idiots of us! You're none other than Sultana Medjahed. Sultana, Sultana, ha, ha! Sultana from what? Like mother, like daughter! You, you make a fuss with me, but you sleep with the Kabyle and the roumi. When you were younger you were already sleeping with the roumis. Who was the first one to have you? That doctor named Challes, huh? We watched you go by, we did, your nose turned up, and we swore to live it up with you, a handful of real sons of the ksar. One day we'll do it to you, you'll see!'

The same pus drops in the corners of his eyes. Undoubtedly, the same fly on the pus. On his back, the same torn jacket. The same hate that twists his face and tortures his nervous tics. And me, the same person, too. The same Sultana. Always early or late. Never in the present, never self-assured in my retorts. Marbah starts his car again and leaves squawking and gesticulating in a cacophony of disjointed movements. I remain, the dagger of the insult in my heart, watching the car move away. Anger comes to me only afterward, too late.

I run toward the hospital and slam the door behind me. Within these walls I've always found a sense of peace and security, a moment apart. I stop in the entryway panting, with my nose at bay. Something is missing in the atmosphere to which I'd become reaccustomed: the smell of coffee, which generally covers the stench of various medical products and the voices talking and responding to each other, above the violins of groans in the waiting rooms. This silence frightens me, threatens me.

'Khaled!'

No answer. He must be visiting the in-patient wing, I say to myself. I look at my watch. It's only five after seven! Khaled doesn't arrive for another half hour, to start the morning rounds with his two assistants. What to do with all this time until nine-thirty, the beginning of consultations? There are no patients who can justify my presence so early.

I leave. The morning light is an iridescent mauve color on the still sleepy village. I realize that I'm heading toward the old neighborhoods. Then I retreat inwardly from everything except this strange sensation of turning things over in my mind in a state of worried sleepwalking.

Suddenly, something pulls me from this state. I recognize the house of my childhood. My body stiffens as hard as steel. I bend it. I break it. I stack it and sit down in front of a gaping threshold. There's no longer a door there or anywhere in the vicinity. For the most part, the walls and the roofs have caved in. Why did I come here this morning? Because that devilish Marbah spoke violently about my mother?

After the death of my mother, my uncle had rented the house. That had seemed to me to be a violation. I wanted it to be intact and its drama sealed within it forever. Sometimes I would come by here during the afternoon siesta. I would stop dead in my tracks fearfully, convinced that my mother, my sister, and the child in me, dead along with them, were staring at me from the cracks between the door's planks. Then I was submerged by ambiguous feelings: the desire to rush toward them, to completely join with them and with their fearful flight through the ksar's deserted alleys. I was still unaware of nostalgia, the worst of ambiguities, unaware of the worst violation, the inexorable movement of time that marks you and disperses you – living indicators of a cynical and tyrannical Tom Thumb who never retraces his steps. My uncle ruined my images from years past, destroyed my childhood vistas. The dead women of my family have no more shelter. They've been lost among the diaspora of shadows that haunt masses of fallen rocks and debris.

I take a large detour along the palm grove. Just walk. Walk a long time so as to extinguish all sensation, reach absolute whiteness.

Sitting on the low hospital wall, Vincent is waiting for me. As soon as he sees me, he gets up to greet me.

'Where did you go?'

'I took a walk in the palm grove. Needed to walk.'

'You woke up very early.'

'I think so.'

'Did you sleep well?'

'Yes, enough, and you?'

'Hmm, you didn't notice anything this morning?'

'No. What should I have noticed?'

'In front of the house, both cars' tires are slashed.'

I can't keep from bursting out laughing.

'That's the only effect it has on you?'

'I'd warned you that to show yourself with me would bring you nothing but trouble.'

'That's not true. Last night I was very happy even if . . . weren't you?'

'Me, I content myself with existing. That's already so complicated.'

Why does he suddenly become livid? What hurtful thing did I say?

'Whoever did this must have been driving the car that followed you last night,' he says, looking sullen.

'But the car was gone when you arrived.'

'It certainly came back afterward. What kind of car was it?'

'Oh, am I stupid! I had completely forgotten that important detail.'

'Which one?'

'The car model, of course, where's my head? A model that's impossible to find here. You know, an American type with a huge engine. That had reinforced my feeling that it was unreal.'

'Unreal, I agree. So you're not going to keep insisting that this blasted car was going along all alone without a driver?'

I don't answer.

'Listen, I'm going to try and find some tires. You should get some rest. Please don't work. They'll manage without you. All they have to do is request a doctor from Tammar. Anyway, Salah is of the same opinion as I am.'

'Salah?'

'Yes. Wouldn't you know, he's the one who woke me up a while ago. He was calling for you from Algiers. He must have called you at the hospital too. Maybe he'll come by plane tonight if he can.'

'Why? What'd you tell him?'

'He's worried about you. I only confirmed to him that you seemed exhausted, physically and psychologically.'

'But I'm fine. I swear! What's with you that you all want to take care of me? I'm sick and tired of it!'

His eyes roll with despair. What's happening to him? Love at first sight? That's all I need. Yet I can't resist a certain feeling. So I add more kindly: 'I don't think you can find tires here. You'll have to go to Tammar. Don't take the taxi whose driver has a beard and a white chechia. He's crazy.'

'Could he be the guilty one? Did he threaten you in the past? What kind of car does he have?'

'A 504.'

'He must have another "American-type" . . . he or one of his friends. I'd swear it.'

'All you have to do is take the bus, at least for the trip there. You'll find it over there on the square. And a piece of advice for a piece of advice. I have this one for you: you've come to discover the desert, right? So leave, go travel it up and down, and leave me to my affairs.'

'To your preoccupations, you mean.'

'To my preoccupations, also, yes. Nobody can take them on or solve them for me.'

'Undoubtedly, although sometimes . . . as for the desert, I'd like to discover it with you. You also came back for it, didn't you?'

'To tell the truth, I'm not aware of the exact reason or reasons for my return. Everything is so interwoven, confused, in my mind. And anyway, you know, desert freedom, escape, finding yourself . . . those are tourists' baggage. I have others. Very different, alas, and that risk disappointing you. Do you think I'm representative of the people here?'

'Little Dalila, she too is already a solitary being. Yet I'm sure that she must be able to identify with you. I think you're dramatizing a bit. But maybe that's the thing about you that attracts me.'

'Enough of this endless discussion, I have to go to work now.'

'So, I'll see you soon?'

I hide myself in the white of my doctor's coat. I open the door. There are a lot of them. They'll take all my attention, summon me, consolidate me in my role as doctor.

I see a man who has crabs even in his eyebrows and nose hairs.

'You have to wash yourself and apply this product.'

'It can't go away with a shot?'

Good heavens! I'd forgotten the magic effect of the shot on the people from here.

'No, no, no shot for you.'

I see a case of scabies that is so old, so overinfected, that the patient is no more than one big pruritus, a cracking and bleeding scab.

'You must coat yourself with this powder. You must . . .'

I see a man with an anal canker sore, undoubtedly a case of syphilis.

'Are you homosexual?'

'I'm a Muslim.'

'Be careful of AIDS! Ask your partners to put on condoms.'

'I'm a believer. I'm a Muslim!'

'Religiosity doesn't protect you from illness. Faith is not a vaccination.'

'There's only one morality that means anything to me: Muhammad's.'

'Who's talking about morality? It's a matter of prevention.'

'You're not gonna give me a shot?'

'Oh, yes, you bet!'

With pleasure I stick him with a strong dose of Extencillin, a painful injection because of the product itself. But since the pain experienced is considered to be proportional to the hoped-for benefits, he leaves limping but content. The bacteriological analysis will confirm that it's syphilis. I won't see the fellow again.

A bearded patient wants me to heal him without having to examine him. He beats around the bush, staring at the wall above my head.

'I'm a doctor, not a sorceress. I have to examine you.'

'You're a woman. You can't touch me. It's a sin . . .'

'So get out of here!'

'You're not gonna give me a shot?'

'For that, you'd consent to hand over one of your buns, you who don't even dare to look at me, right?'

'It's the shot that touches me, it's not you.'

'Well, you won't have that little treat. Get out of here, I've had enough of your bargaining!'

I see another bearded guy with all the humility and kindness of the poor, and whose beard is only something borrowed from the stinking prowling zoo, with no true meaning.

'I have to tell you, tabiba, the only thing that cures me is a shot.'

A little bit of distilled water in an intramuscular shot lights up his happy child's face. He folds his prescription so many times that it ends up resembling a talisman. He places it in the pocket of his gandoura, against his heart. I'm almost certain he won't go buy the medications. Undoubtedly too expensive for his pocketbook. A piece of writing against his heart and the intrusion of some iron into his skin are enough to outsmart the day's illness. He must have baraka![1]

I see a third bearded patient who undresses without any fuss. As I palpate his abdomen, his kohl-adorned eyes palpate me from head to foot, hungrily, shamelessly.

I see a haggard and terrorized eleven-year-old girl:

'I think my face has yellowed.'

'Your face has yellowed? You're not yellow. You have a normal beautiful tanned complexion.'

'No, no,' she weakly protests, 'it's because my stepmother always says to me, "May God make your face yellow!" I mean, may he take away my dignity.'

'You mean your virginity?'

'Yes. She wishes it on me so often, so often, that I'm already afraid I've lost it, my dignity, and that everyone in the village, they'll see it on my yellowed face.'

'You can't lose your virginity just because of your stepmother's incantations and curses!'

I need time to reassure her and also make her understand that her chastity and her hymen don't risk anything in the hammam, another source of panic, except for losing their filth;[2] that a sperm is not caught by sitting in the nude where, a few instants earlier, a nude man sat, nor is it caught like a virus, by a mere change in the ambient temperature.

Her anguish about her 'dignity' remains, obviously, out of my reach. Even a shot can't do anything for her.

I see a young girl, her face turned away and who doesn't make a peep. The woman accompanying her has an abnormally rigid face. Her words

1. Baraka: luck.
2. Hammam: public baths, also a place to socialize and converse.

and gestures are few, broken. At the moment I greet them, Khaled motions to me.

'Can you come to the infirmary for a moment?'

I follow him.

'The girl was impregnated by her brother. It's a problem of promiscuity, among others. There are thirteen brothers and sisters living in a two-room place. Their father died a few years ago. When the mother realized her daughter was pregnant, she took her to the north. They came back after the birth, alone. It's said that the mother may have killed her daughter's baby. Since then, the girl has become mute and the mother is stiff, trembling, and she stutters. A calamity with no solution!'

Such profound and complicated koulchites as this would necessitate that the needle search in the blood and inject directly the antidote for the 'stain.' Their eyes, where I can see that the drama has settled forever, tell me that mine would be a superfluous gesture.

I see an acute koulchite, an inflammation of the soul and the being in a sixteen-year-old girl. She has just married. I see a chronic koulchite, a mute and gangrenous cry from the daily existence of a prolific mother: eleven children and the husband still doesn't want to hear a word about birth control. I see a terminal koulchite, a heart churning emptily in a clay body. It's a forty-year-old woman with no children. I see a hysterical koulchite . . . a shot of Valium for this one, tailor-made injections for the others.

I see several teenagers with heart conditions resulting from untreated cases of angina. They, for whom penicillin is absolutely necessary over long periods of time, come for the 'shot' appointments only in a folkloric manner, regularity not being a habit in these climes. When poverty is exacerbated by ignorance, the most common ailment evolves into something incurable and deadly. There are places where life is never anything but a vicious death that delights in itself and takes its time.

I see. I poke. I sew. I see. I poke. I plaster. I see. I poke. I cut. The blotting paper in me drinks. When they've all left, the sting of their pain is in me, shooting. The stench of their distress smothers the atmosphere. The office has on me the effect of an overcrowded trench. I open the window. Dead souls escape like smoke. The burst of the sky is devilish laughter that sweeps away the last groans.

Sky negation, lamenting, concentrated misery, the sky doesn't give a damn. The wind's hysteria, orgies of silence, it doesn't give a damn. The bragging sun that burns itself up because it doesn't have anything else to burn, it doesn't give a damn. The whirlwind of sand that rustles and simpers, the prowling night that covers the stars in ink, don't give a damn. The theatrical night, which believes itself fatal, which darkens or beautifies itself behind a moon with a madam's smile. The weather-beaten day, the damned day, its hallucinations, its mirages, the day torn between abyss and blazing fire, it doesn't give a damn. It covers human decay with an unchangeable arrogance.

I'd also like to be able not to give a damn. I can't manage it. Is it because the suffering of others is for me a medication? Because their string of moans relieves me from myself? Undoubtedly, because, really, I am no Samaritan spirit.

Khaled comes into my office with a worried look.

'You did well to open the window up wide,' he says, his mind obviously elsewhere.

He hands me a cigarette. I accept it.

'Is something wrong, Khaled?'

'Aren't you hungry?'

'No, thank you.'

'When do you eat?'

'Oh, I ate a little this morning.'

'Do you know what time it is?'

I look at my watch. It says three-thirty.

'Ya lalla, with Yacine and the doctors before, we sent people home about twelve-thirty and told them to return about two-thirty.[1] We took

1. *Ya lalla:* Oh, madam.

the time to eat and rest a little. You're going to kill yourself, kill us with your exhausting all-day-long schedule.'

'Excuse me, Khaled. I didn't think of that. But starting tomorrow we'll adopt your usual hours. I put you in charge of reminding me. Is that all right? Do you want to do it that way?'

'Okay. Come and eat in the infirmary. My wife sent us a gumbo tajine.'

I don't want to upset him further. I follow him to the infirmary. His dish is already heating. While he sets up dishes and silverware on a little table, he says to me, trying to be light-hearted, but nevertheless tense:

'You haven't used it yet, but you have a car available to you in the hospital garage. The keys are in the right-hand drawer of your desk. It's best to lock it inside at night. They're not going to leave you alone. Now that I know who you are, I think that Salah was right to oppose your staying in Aïn Nekhla. Even though he knew nothing about you and your family, people's mentalities haven't evolved. On the contrary, they've become entrenched. Here, a woman like you is in even more danger than before.'

'Today is really my day . . . So you know who I am?'

'Yes. They do too, and in a few hours the entire village will know. They'll make sure of that.'

They. Everybody here says *they* when they're talking about members of the FIS. *They*, all at once grasshoppers, smallpox, typhus, cancer, leprosy, plague, and AIDS of the mind. *They*, an endemic disease that has burst from the confines of misery and confusion, and that encysts in the fatality and ignorance of the country.

'*They* don't scare me! Whatever label they may wear now, it's never a matter of anything but the faces of hatred from my childhood. Regimes and political parties live, wear themselves out, and die. Misogyny stays and feeds and strengthens itself from failure.'

'The mayor, Bakkar, came by an hour ago. He hasn't stopped thundering forth and ruminating, "She dares come here! She came to thumb her nose at me, huh? We'll see about that!"'

'Still as full of himself and as boastful as ever, that one. If he comes back again, warn me. I'll throw him out.'

[109]

'Watch out, these people are violent. And now that they have a bit of power, they think they're allowed to do anything . . . Salah called this morning before going to the operating room.'

'Is he doing well?'

'He's indestructible, amazing.'

He eats. I pick at my food and chew, unable to swallow. He pretends not to notice. I'm grateful to him.

Memories come back to me from the time when I helped Paul Challes. To try and cheer up Khaled, I tell him how I'd realized, while listening to patients, that the first suppositories ever distributed had been dissolved in tea and drunk; that the ophthalmic ointments had been taken by the teaspoon and forced down with sips of tea, because 'it was impossible to swallow them in any other way!'

We've just finished the in-patient rounds when Salah bursts into the lobby. 'Hi, gang!' he cries out to no one in particular, with a somewhat forced joviality. Then, in my direction: 'How's it going? The load's not too heavy?'

'No, no. I was worried about the maternity ward, but the midwives have completely taken over for me. I asked them to contact the gynecologist in Tammar in case of problems. They'll carry out the routine work.'

When we're alone in the office, his yellow eyes light up with anger. He attacks: 'Do you look at yourself in the mirror once in a while?'

'Why, should I?'

'Yes, you should! You have ugly shadows under your eyes and an ashen complexion. Your face is gaunt. You must have lost ten or twelve pounds in three days. Since you didn't have any extra . . .'

'Listen, I've had enough!'

'You've had enough, you've had enough! You're letting yourself perish and you're working at making the village rise up against you. Where do you want to go with this?'

'The village against me? That's nothing new! The difference is that I'm no longer a powerless child! I'm going to watch how the rest of the hostilities turn out. Do you forget that the fact that we slept under the same roof has set everything off again?'

He lowers his head and looks at me from beneath his stubborn forehead. 'Under the same roof, but not in the same bed. Maybe that's my problem. I'm certainly jealous, but I'm also worried about you. Why do you say "set off again?" The village's hostility toward you isn't something new? What do you have to settle with this village?'

'That's not your business. On the other hand, yes, in spite of all your beautiful challenges to society, if you want to let your daily behavior be dictated by ignoramuses, you're free to. But for pity's sake, spare me your warnings!'

'It's not a matter of letting myself be dictated to! In the name of God, do you understand that we live in an explosive time? Do like the other Algerian women, the real ones . . .'

'The real! The real ones! Always this same word! Do more false, more underhanded qualifiers than that one exist?'

'You always split hairs with words, like a Western woman. I'm only asking you to behave like a responsible and intelligent woman. The women here are all in the resistance. They know that they can't attack head-on an almost totally unjust and monstrous society. So they have taken to the underground of knowledge, of work, and of financial autonomy. They're persevering in the shadow of men who stagnate and despair. They don't lapse into useless and dangerous provocation, like you. They pretend and hide, not just to avoid being crushed, but to continue advancing.'

'This resistance of theirs that you describe gives them momentum and structure. For me, I would have needed a big dose of hate to hold on and stay here. Hatred incites you, gets your back up, fixes you and arms you. In its grip, you defend yourself, you take vengeance. The lack of hatred gives you no opening, except into flight and wandering. And also, "real Algerian women" don't have a problem with their identity. They're from an epoch, a land. They're whole. I've been many-faceted and torn apart since childhood. That's only been aggravated with age and exile. In France now, I'm neither Algerian nor even North African. I'm an Arab. That's as much as to say nothing. Arab, this word dissolves you in the grayness of a nebula. Here, I'm no longer Algerian, nor am I French. I wear a mask. A Western mask? The mask of an émigré? The height of the paradox is that the two often merge. By virtue of always being elsewhere, you inevitably become different. Whether you are interesting, interrogating, or shocking, you are a moving peculiarity in time, in space, and in the diverse ideas that people can create out of "the foreigner." But would you believe that as uncomfortable as this foreign skin can be sometimes, it's nonetheless an invaluable source of freedom. I wouldn't exchange it for anything in the world! Also, I never hide anything. And the rumors and criticisms generally do nothing but urge on the jubilation that all transgressions provide me with.'

Salah is quiet for a moment. He masters his vehemence, leans his elbows on the desk, and with his hands in his chin, stares at me with his cat eyes where a golden magic spell shines forth. Then little by little an ironic smile forms on his lips. He admits, biting his lip, 'I thought I was going to die this morning when that guy answered the phone in place of you, hearing him get alarmed about you, yawning in your bed. It's an intolerable and idiotic way to realize that you're in love.'

Troubled, I get out of it with a pirouette: 'You know, a slightly libertine nurse at the hospital in Oran told me one day about a lover who was becoming too invasive for her taste: "Why is that guy after me! I didn't take anything from him. We kissed each other and each of us kept our lips!" For a long time I've made that my motto.'

He pulls me into the yellow of his eyes. From his angry silence arises my desire. I'll always be surprised by the body's resources.

'You mean that you never get attached, don't you? Is that possible?'

'I've had my share of lovers, yet I've always lost them on paths with no return. I'm never left with anything but a gaping, unsatisfied desire.'

'There you are starting to talk like a book again!'

I burst out laughing. He laughs too.

His frankness, his face, his arms, his large body, I like everything about him. His eyes are amber-colored intoxication. Yet my desire quickly dissipates. Why does he become so changeable, so ephemeral? I observe Salah and say to myself that this return to my country could have been one of love found again: Salah or Vincent . . . But this floating sensation leaves me without an anchor in reality. As if this realization of the impossibility of a true return had consumed my other desires, had disembodied me. My punctual body evaporated. The others, dispersed in my varied strangeness, are no longer anything but far-off dreams, as if unfulfilled. It is insidious, this feeling of an impossible return, in spite of the return. The inability to find this 'lost space' expels you from the present and from yourself. I would like to try to dissect this feeling of loss so as to annihilate it. But I feel it to be so confused and buried that it discourages me. Suddenly I feel so listless.

'Come with me to Algiers or, if you prefer, leave for Oran. You'll quickly find a job there. You won't stand out for any reason from the great mass of active women. Don't stay here. A village like this one is a trap that risks closing on you.'

'I want to stay in Aïn Nekhla for a while. It gives me a feeling of usefulness that I need right now. Afterward, I'll return to Montpellier.'

'But you can have the feeling of usefulness everywhere else in the country. I don't understand why you persist in this way. I'm starting to say to myself that Yacine and even his death were just pretexts. What did you come looking for here? You don't want to reveal to me what dispute you have with this village?'

'But I assure you, I have none . . . Do you know that Yacine's and Vincent's car tires were slashed last night?'

'You see! This is just a warning. Next time they'll go after you. They've thrown acid at girls just because of their clothing. You and your thoughtless behavior!'

'Enough. Tell me instead how Algiers is.'

'Bad. Algiers has the sad and dirty face of an orphan. More and more shaggy beards and women transformed into ravens or nuns. I, who hated haïks, now I'm almost nostalgic for them.[1] At least they weren't devoid of eroticism. Bab el-Oued and the Casbah are endlessly distended and fermenting bellies.[2] Anguished twitches show on everyone's faces. Algiers is an immense psychiatric ward, abandoned with no caretaker, and which knows only the language of violence.'

I mention files I have to complete, X-ray reports and lab analyses to look at, so as not to have to accompany Salah to Yacine's. He goes there alone. I let myself go in the silence.

The air is bitingly fresh. I tighten my sweater around my neck. What did I do with my scarf? The west is burning in the sunset's fire. In the south, a chestnut-colored cloud rises and moves forth with the gait of a giant. Is it the sand wind? Emotion seizes me and stops me in front of the hospital. I return to the office. I grab the keys that Khaled told me about. I run toward the garage in the back of the building. The hospital car is a Renault 4. It starts with the first try of the key. I leave the village and soon afterward the paved road. I fly toward the south.

The car is tossed about on the erg's pebbles. In the desert, a vehicle is nothing but a cockroach. Cockroach jumps, grasshopper jumps without wings or radar. My foot accelerating and accelerating changes nothing. Glued to the window, the desert beats down on me, mocks me with its nothingness. Fundamentalist, macabre desert that pretends to be dead and waits for the red orgasm of the wind. Lascivious dune. Its breasts gorged with the sun. The harlot dune, offered, and whose immobility breathes in the wind. Dune, flower of an arid desire. The stones, the erg's tears, solid despair encrusting itself in the smallest span of earth. The stones flow and roll on eternity's mournful display.

The wind approaches. I cut the engine, open my window. The abyss of si-

1. *Haïk:* a long piece of rectangular-shaped material worn by Muslim women over their other clothes.

2. Bab el-Oued: a neighborhood in Algiers. Casbah: originally, a citadel or palace, or the neighborhood surrounding it. The Casbah of Algiers is known for its traditional-style architecture and winding, seemingly endless streets and alleys.

lence makes me momentarily dizzy. A dizziness that fills, little by little, the wind's upsurge. Panting. Murmuring. Protests. Anger and roaring. Then a blade of sand crashes down on everything. An end-of-the-world cataclysm.

I cough, spit out sand, close the window. The car pitches, grates, whistles. The car body emits acid hisses. Dust infiltrates all the way into my lungs.

People are mere fleas living as parasites in the desert. It cleanses itself of them in the trances of Aeolus. In this celestial breath, the desert is a sublime insanity to be lived, a joyful death straddling the world. Glory to its reddish cavalcade.

All of a sudden, there in front of me, headlights pierce the wind's impenetrable hysteria. I turn on the Renault 4's lights. I only see these headlights in the demonic mass of the sand's turmoil. But when the breakers lessen their force, I perceive the outline of a big-engined car.

I open my window, stick my head out, and with my eyes closed, yell, 'Who are you?'

The wind mocks me. The wind bites into me and swallows my words.

'Who are you?'

The wind slaps me. It whistles and with a wall of sand buries me alive. I close the window again, cough, blow my nose. I have sand all the way into my brain. My thoughts crunch. My eyes cry and sting. I wipe them. I don't see anything anymore. The headlights reappear through my tears, right in front of me. Their light bursts like lightning and sparkles in my tears. The headlights are big globular eyes being gnawed by the storm's cataracts, big toad eyes blinking their sand eyelids.

'Who are you? What do you *too* want from me?'

The car trembles. The wind belches and haunts me. The wind carries me away. The wind becomes confused. A lover who cannot be grasped but who makes me drunk with his joy.

'Are you Yacine?'

The wind scolds me, brutalizes the car.

'Are you . . .'

Is it possible that there's no one in the car? I'd like to go see. But I have neither the force nor the courage to do so.

[115]

8

VINCENT

I'll take her with me on the boat. I'll take her to the cradle of the seas. I already see the weather vane that pierces the skies, the keel, sliding and cleaving a blue desire, the great calm that hangs suspended from the sails, creasing their cloth and smoothing down liquid secrets, slowing secrets, the shimmering stretched between faraway places and our dreams. We'll go to Folegandros, where peace is perched on high, a village coiled up around its white solitude, like a shell thrown by an angry sea to the tip of an arid island. We'll go to Amorgos, where a cove offers a place to anchor, hidden even from the tourists. I'll take her to Kos for a brief pilgrimage to the foot of Hippocrates' tree. Then we'll flee from this place where, in the summer, the beer drowns the ouzo, where blond mops of hair unfurl with the Meltemi. We'll avoid the other places with all the tourists. We'll make our way toward the most isolated stones of the Cyclades to meet the gods in their blustery summits. With the water's thread, my love will weave its desires.

Now when I awake, I think about her first, think about her for a long time. Only afterward do I think of my kidney. And still it's less a worry than a habit, less a caress than a precaution. Now I have a hard-on every morning.

A piece of flesh has liberated me from a machine. I have healed because of it. A woman, a love, are saving me from myself, healing me from my transplant and from the paradoxical feeling of a remedy derived from mutilation. I was nothing but a presence/absence, filled with relief/with a feeling of having taken on an irreversible debt, with the anguish of death/the desire to live, soldered in an endless state of body to body, an endless convalescence. To have had a brush with death and to have avoided it is a miracle that plunges you into a shaky and fearful state of euphoria. Some time is absolutely necessary to finally reach a total state of strength. Love is my cure.

Be careful with this guy Salah! An intelligent and handsome kid, what's more. Not convenient, this morning on the phone. Only in the beginning, to tell the truth. He softened afterward. At the sound of his voice, I grabbed my kidney like a cowboy on guard who feverishly moves his hand to his gun. But me, I only draw my assurance, my insolence or my laziness, accordingly.

Then, unconsciously, my fingers recognized the limits of my transplant, by its contours devoid of sensation. The transplant has this about it; paradoxically, it occupies the mind in vain, makes it obsessed, but the nerve endings of the receiver's body never settle into the transplanted kidney. Such that one can have a fever and even begin to reject the organ without ever feeling the slightest pain in the transplant. The only sign of pathology that the latter can show is a swelling, like a silent discontentment, when the organ becomes recalcitrant. Thus the kidney is felt only by touch and by the metamorphosis brought about in us. As if, to the perfect 'tissue identity' that would like to fully blend into the receiver's body, the donor opposed an insurmountable resistance, a stubbornness to remain another sensibility, a foreign particle, an anesthetized zone, thus erasing the recipient. And in spite of the drugs that diminish immunity, the kidney is, truly and inescapably, little by little absorbed until the last stage of rejection. In this way a third kidney meets the fate of one's own kidneys. A few grams of supplementary death and the swing toward a more severe stage of the illness.

But it seems that our complete tissue identity keeps my transplant and me from such a fate. It seems. 'You, you have your kidney for life! Look at what you need in terms of immunosuppressants. Next to nothing!' argued the medical corps in reaction to my fears and skepticism. The 'next to nothing' appears to me to be considerable in this case: daily pills. The same goes for the transplant as with any integration of a 'foreigner.' The work of reciprocal acceptance is necessary: chemical work exerted by pharmaceutical remedies on the patients' bodies, for one, pedagogical remedies on the social body, for the other.

Even in Tammar, I didn't find tires. Distraught, I sought help from Tayeb, the restaurant owner.

'You come back at about seven in the evening, you'll have tires for your car. I don't know about the other.'

'But how will you get them? I went to see all the mechanics.'

'Hey, my family, the familial Algerian getting by, you know!'

After hanging around in the souk, I went for my rendezvous with Moh.

'So, you did your work?'

'Uhh . . . yes, yes.'

'Your work, it was to wait for a woman who takes herself for a movie ichira?'

'Ichira?'

'You say "star." '

'But how do you know all that? You spied on me?'

'Personally, I don't need to spy on you. Here, we're so disgusted and bored with ourselves that everybody watches everybody. We have to.'

'Bored?'

He puts his hands around his neck and squeezes, expressing asphyxiation. Then, relaxing: 'Here, all the young people are disgusted and bored . . . So did you do your business with her?'

'I don't "do my business" with anyone. And anyway, what business is it of yours?'

'You're right to make the most of it. You're a man!'

From this air of fraternal indulgence, I guess that his estimation of me, lowered by my refusal to accompany him to the brothel, has gone up again. The dinner at his home is a feast. The dessert of mint tea and date cake is too. Afterward, I return to the hotel, where I doze off.

When I awake, I decide to wait for Dalila before going again to Tayeb's.

I'm leaving the hotel when I see her climbing up the dune. Once on the top I follow her footprints and find her behind a sand dune.

'Are you hiding now?'

'Yes, because of all the roaming eyes.' Then, after a moment of silence and a glance toward the erg: 'She left again.'

'You don't want to tell me who she is?'

'I can't tell you.'

'Why?'

'I can't tell you!' Then, cheerfully and with an engaging look: 'But I'd like it a lot if you'd say another word with space in it, like "peut-être."'[1]

'I thought you didn't appreciate that word.'

'Yesterday I looked at it for a long time in the dictionary. Above it, there's "fearful." That one, I hate it. Below it, there's a lot of words I've never seen, never heard. Now I find it pretty, this word with its "peut" that has a head and a tail and its "être" that has a hat behind its head. And the dash that unifies the two and makes it look like they're holding their hands to walk.'

'Hmm, hmm, does it happen that you often consult the dictionary?'

'Consult? The dictionary's not a doctor!'

'. . . Yes it is, a little bit. It's the language doctor. It heals mistakes. It takes care of wounded words.'

Burst of laughter.

'Do you often use it?'

'Yes. Before, I stole it from Ouarda and hid so I could read it. But Ouarda saw me and said I could take it as long as I don't mess it up. I read a lot of pages. Even when I don't understand everything, it works my head. You'll give me another word with some space?'

1. *Peut-être:* maybe.

'Well . . . doubt, for example.'

'Yes, that one, I saw it in the dictionary, too, in the explanation of "maybe." It's sort of its ex aequo brother.'

'Memory?'

'Memory, it's when you learn well at school. Memory's space isn't it?'

'Obviously, and it's not only what you can learn at school. It's . . . it's time's film and its events.'

'You speak the way Lamartine writes,' she interrupts dryly.

It's my turn to burst out laughing. She stares at me with eyes stirred by a mocking mischievousness.

'Do you read Lamartine?'

'Yes. Ouarda, she has me learn Lamartine, Musset, Victor Hugo, Senghor, Omar Khayyam, Imru'al-Qays, and even others.'

'That's good! Memory, it's what you remember of the world and of your own life in this world, past and present.'

'So it's all your memories?'

'Yes, all.'

'Even the ones you forget?'

'Yes, even those. One day, boom! They come back to you like migratory birds.'

'Migratory birds are sun and freedom trabendists. I'd like to live like them. Memories, they're not all pretty. But I don't like forgetting.'

'Yet it's also a space.'

'I don't like forgetting. Forgetting, it's a hole. It rewinds you backward. Forgetting is a word from the earth.'

'It's a necessary word.'

My assertion makes her face cloud over. I try to find a word of reconciliation.

'Hey . . . let's see, another word that has space . . . love? Well, yes, love is an immense space, sublime.'

'Love, it's pretty, very pretty. But with us, it's like the clouds, there aren't many. With us, even the government is afraid of women. It makes laws against them. So love is just shame, which is nationally elected. Another

[120]

time in Ouarda's secondary school, a twelve-year-old boy wrote "I love you" on a piece of paper and he had it passed to a girl. Immediately it was like a coup . . . How do you say it?'

'How do you say what?'

'A coup to kill the government, how do you say that?'

'A coup d'état?'

'Yes, like a coup d'état. And the secondary school Scotland Yard, they found the "guilty one." They insulted him and punished him. On TV they always cut out the love kisses in the films. The ones with a satellite dish hook-up, they're lucky. They see love kisses from LaFrance.'

'You don't like shame, do you, huh?'

'No. Tradition just threatens girls. And if you don't obey, it makes your brothers' and father's faces fall, and they become broken necks. Because a lot of girls and women, a lot of men, they're just broken necks.'

'Broken necks?'

'Yes, when they have h'chouma from their girls or wife, they can't go out anymore, in front of other men, with their heads up. They become broken necks. A broken neck, you catch it quickly and it doesn't heal.'

'You know, expressed or not, love exists everywhere, only sometimes it's a little bit like your eyes, you don't see it, you see with it.'

'Maybe it's the way you say it is, in your home in LaFrance. Here, love, it's only in songs. People drink tea and listen to the songs. And they're so beaten down by everything that's impossible. So they don't talk. They swallow their hot sadness with their tea. Me, I don't have h'chouma, I have anger with claws. I don't look at the ground. I look people in the eye. And when I'm sick of their rotted eyes, I come here and I look at dreams to clean mine. My sister, Samia, says that we Algerian girls, we're all "Alice in Merguezland"; since we never have wonders, we put spices everywhere, everywhere.[1] Dreams are my spices. Boys, when they're not Islamists or broken necks, they're just Aldo Macciones without flouss.'[2]

1. *Merguez:* a very spicy sausage eaten in Algeria.
2. *Flouss:* money.

[121]

'You mean they're all machos, they all race cars like Maccione?'

'Yes, machos. But Aldo Maccione, he does that to play in films. They do that for real. They sway their shoulders and flex their muscles like camels and they mimic rajla, but they're only fachla.[1] That means they're not machos 'cause they're brave, or they work or study, no, they're just clothes machos, they don't work and they bug women.'

'Well!'

'You know . . .'

'Yes?'

She hesitates an instant before admitting: 'Yesterday, I had a horrible dream while I was sleeping.' Her eyes sparkling, she bursts out laughing.

'A nightmare?'

'Can there be a beautiful nightmare that you like? . . . I dreamed I was the Tin Drum, a girl Tin Drum. I was walking down the streets of Tammar, pounding on the drum. I was pounding and pounding. In the street, the men and the boys were looking at me. And all the eyes glued on me. I was yelling at them loudly, very loudly. It was making their eyes burst like glass breaking. Their faces were funny looking, with red holes instead of eyes. And me, I was laughing. And my voice blew out more and more eyes. Pop! Pop! Pop! Like when women throw salt in the fire to burn the evil eye. It goes pop, pop, pop.'

'You know, you should draw or paint these images that come into your head.'

'The images don't come! I'm the one who looks for them and finds them!' she cries out. 'And anyway, I've been drawing since I was really little.'

'What do you draw?'

'A lot of eyes. Madam Tradition twisted up by old-fashioned ideas. Blessing that prays falsely and evil that menaces and makes faces. H'chouma, with its stomach where fears are like death worms. And even more and more . . . things that are so mean they're funny. Ouarda, she says "ferocious."'

1. *Rajla*: men. *Fachla*: weak.

[122]

'So you have to continue.'

'I'm afraid they'll say: "She's crazy. She's possessed by Bliss!" '

'You mustn't show your drawings to just anyone. I'm sure that Ouarda won't think so, she won't.'

'Yacine already told me that. But you need a lot of colors to draw well. I don't have the money to buy them.'

'I'd be very pleased to give them to you.'

'Yacine also wanted to. But how can I trick my parents?'

'We'll have to arrange it so they know nothing. What's most important is that you can draw when you want to.'

She looks toward the dunes with a dejected face.

'Soon I'll be too big. A big girl can't come and dream on a dune. Yacine had promised me he'd go see Ouarda and become her friend and speak to her about the drawings. But he died.'

'I'll go see Ouarda in his place.'

'You can give me that if you want. But it'll be more difficult for you. You're a roumi.'

Suddenly she bursts into sobs. In a mix of hiccups and sniffles, she excuses herself. 'I'm not crying because you're a roumi. That doesn't matter. I'm crying for Yacine.'

Tayeb found me four tires.

'The others, in two days if you want. It's better that I buy them for you. With your roumi face, the bastards will make you pay five times as much.'

I refuse the taxi whose driver is bearded and wearing a chechia. 'Yan âl dinn oumek!' he shouts out.[1]

I don't know what that means. Not friendly, obviously. In my opinion, he must take his junk heap for an airplane. Without a doubt because of the racket it makes. He takes off, blinding me with dust.

After a moment of waiting, I load my tires into another taxi, which drives me toward Aïn Nekhla.

---

1. *Yan âl dinn oumek!:* Cursed be your mother's religion!

It's already dark, but 'whore,' written in large letters on Sultana's door, stands out. It's Salah who opens the door.

'Vincent Chauvet?'

'Yes, good evening.'

'Good evening, I'm Salah Akli. Isn't Sultana with you?'

'No, no, I haven't seen her since this morning.'

'She hasn't returned yet. I called the hospital. They said she'd left around seven-thirty. It's eight-thirty!'

'Maybe she went to see a patient.'

'Alas, here it's always the ill person who is moved, in whatever condition.'

Then, noticing that I'm staring at the word on the door: 'War has been declared. She's going to have to be careful.'

He discovers my tires, grimaces with compassion, and helps me bring them in.

'There's a nice mechanic in the village who'll be able to put them on for you. Tell him I sent you.'

I acquiesce. We look at each other suspiciously.

'Sit down, please,' he finally says. 'It seems to me I've already seen you somewhere.'

'Yes, three days ago at the hotel in Tammar.'

'Ah, yes, that's it . . . Do you want a shot of whiskey? I know Sultana has some.'

'Yes, I'd like some, thank you.'

He brings a bottle and glasses and serves us.

'Excuse me just a moment, I'm going to go finish making something to eat.'

I follow him to the kitchen.

'Where can she be at this hour?'

'She didn't go see little Dalila, in any case.'

'Do you also know Dalila?'

'Yes.'

'Yacine had every intention of helping that child. He was crazy about her. It seems she's very good at sketching. I'd so much like to give her what she needs to draw with, as well as a few books and dictionaries. She also possesses the art of making the best "mixes" of spicy languages.'

'She's conquered you too, from what I can see. We'll have to find a subterfuge.'

He smiles, now completely relaxed.

'Mmm, that's coriander.'

'Yes, with the evening's coolness I suddenly wanted a chorba.[1] I thought Sultana would also like it.'

Suddenly one of the windowpanes smashes into pieces. Consternation. A stone shatters another pane. Immobile, we stare, stupefied, at the glass debris on the ground. Salah is the first to get hold of himself. Throwing his knife into the kitchen sink, he dashes toward the door. I run after him. Outside, a few cries, then a stampede dissolves into the night. We stop.

'Bastards! Damned cowards!' yells Salah.

It's useless to shout at the top of our lungs. They're already far away. We return to the house.

'We have to close all the shutters. Those shits can come back. In the name of God, where is Sultana?'

'But who are those people, Islamists?'

'Islamists or not, there are so many neurotic and repressed people in this country. Before, it was only the party members, the pigs and the orderlies who poisoned our lives. Now, with the decay of the state's authority, any imbecile believes he's invested with a divine right and claims he can mete out justice according to his principles! Moronic populism and nationalism, these are the lifeblood of today's Algeria. Do you want to wait for Sultana here? I'm going to go see if she isn't somewhere in the village.'

'I'll go with you.'

---

1. *Chorba:* a prized soup made of vegetables, lamb, and vermicelli.

There are few street lamps, but the beginning of a moon lights our way sufficiently.

'The nurse, Khaled, told me she had left in the hospital car, a white Renault four ... Did you notice how the temperature plunged this evening, as soon as the sun disappeared?'

'Yes, it's surprising.'

'During the day we're roasted, during the night we're frozen. It's one of the particularities of the desert.'

The streets are empty. A few adolescents hug each other here and there in front of the doors of the houses. When we arrive in front of the mosque, a stream of men are coming out. Their murmurs spread through the street.

'Algeria is swarming with holier-than-thous and prophets of the Apocalypse. Violence and greed are competing with helplessness and insecurity,' mutters Salah, as if for himself.

Some of the men come to a halt and turn around as we go by. I feel the same anxiety and the same uneasiness as I did last night at the hotel.

'Maybe we should ask people whether they've seen her around here.'

'That wouldn't be doing her a favor. Our presence here has already put a curse on her. Oh, what the hell!'

He calls out to several adolescents as we continue moving. Nobody has seen Sultana.

'Listen, you have to help me convince her to leave here. Now that he knows who she is, Khaled is also worried about her. During her childhood Sultana must have lived through a traumatic event, I'm not sure what; Khaled says nothing about it, for which I'm grateful. But he did say that in the past she suffered because of the mentality of the village people. It's always like that when a defenseless girl becomes food for the obsessive fear of The Sin in places where archaic beliefs seem unchangeable. Who can foresee what these minds, darkened by ignorance, will do once they learn her identity? In our country even the most cowardly become heroic when it's a matter of attacking women. In today's chaotic mess, keeping them in a state of slavery seems to be the only issue about which

Algerians are unanimous, the only consensus in the never-ending dissension of the Arabs.'

'I'd like to take her with me by boat. I think the sea will do her a lot of good.'

My wish stops him dead in his tracks. He turns toward me, stares at me and says with biting laughter: 'Is that all? Is it love at first sight?'

'Yes, I think so.'

'Another one! I warn you, my friend, that I'll defend my chances with her all the way to the end.'

We continue our walk in embarrassed silence. At the edge of the village is the huge dark mass of the abandoned ksar. No Renault 4 in sight. Empty-handed, we retrace our steps.

'Since the two cars, yours and Yacine's, are not working, we have nothing more to do except wait until it pleases her to show up. It's ten o'clock. I hope nothing bad has happened to her.'

Salah seasons his soup with coriander and lowers the flame, and then we leave the kitchen for the living room. With a whiskey in hand, I bury myself in the contemplation of Yacine's paintings. The wall fresco is gripping . . . Suddenly, three light knocks startle us. Both of us rush to the door.

'It's Alilou! What are you doing here, little fellow?'

He's a very brown small boy with jet black eyes. Gesticulating a lot, he speaks to Salah. I don't understand anything he says, because he's speaking in Arabic.

'Sultana is in the ksar. He says he followed her and that she's sleeping there now. She's crazy! Alilou heard the big kids say we were searching for her. He came to warn us.'

Salah caresses the boy's head.

'He was also a great friend of Yacine's. People claim he turned dim-witted when he lost his mother more than a year ago, because he spends his time wandering in the ksar and in the dunes. The truth is, Alilou needs solitude. He's a budding artist or poet. Shall we go get her?'

[127]

'Let's go.'

'Wait, we need a flashlight.'

He goes and digs around in the hall closet.

'Okay, we can go.'

Little Alilou takes off ahead of us. When he's a bit too far, he stops, turns around, waits for us, then starts running again when he sees us. We walk fast. We exchange only a few words. Asleep in the ksar? I can't believe it.

A big square separates the inhabited neighborhood from the ksar. The entrance to the alley, by which we enter the ksar, is blocked by a white Renault 4, invisible from the square.

'The hospital car,' proclaims Salah.

The door isn't locked, Salah opens it and notices: 'The keys are in the ignition.'

I don't say a word. Careful of the mass of fallen rocks, Salah joins me again. I follow the little scatterbrained boy prancing about in front of me. The flashlight's beam quickly becomes absolutely necessary in order for us to continue, because the alley narrows and becomes darker and darker. Alilou, used to the place, moves ahead of us. The sound of our steps is muffled by the sand. What on earth can she be doing at this hour in this ghostly and silent ksar?

'Why would she be here at night?' I cry out, defeated by the great anguish overflowing in me.

Little Alilou turns back, bursting into the flashlight's beam: 'Ssshhh!' he says, in a reedy voice.

The anxiety that I read in Salah's eyes augments my own. Alilou turns to the right and gets ahead of us in what must have been a dead end. The wall at the end has caved in. A tomblike silence crushes the darkness. The boy comes to a halt in front of a doorway. The beam of light sweeps across a small courtyard cluttered with the debris of earthen bricks and corncobs. Suddenly, Sultana appears in the light. A terrible cry explodes in me. She is sitting in the middle of the rubble. Her wide-open eyes are frighteningly and incredibly empty.

Taken aback, Salah and I observe her. Then Salah kneels, shakes her, rubs her, slaps her. She doesn't move a muscle. I move him away from her. He collapses next to her. I take off my jacket and make her put it on. She doesn't react. Salah puts his arms around her and clasps her tightly against him. She doesn't move. I pull her away from him and, seizing her, make her get up. Salah helps me. We hold her up until we reach the car, then until we reach the house. She is shivering and her teeth are chattering. In the light her face is blotchy from the cold and her eyes unfathomable.

'I'm going to make a fire in the living room. There's a bit of wood behind the house,' says Salah.

We place Sultana in front of the fire and take turns feeding her chorba. She doesn't resist us at all but only swallows occasionally, like a sort of intermittent automatic functioning, in spite of her total emptiness.

After the chorba, we make her drink as many spoonfuls of whiskey as we can, while at the same time deadening ourselves with it. Then we put her to bed on the sofa and tuck her in, arguing over pieces of the bedding.

It seems to us that, little by little, her eyes look less lost, less far-off. At first we attribute this only to the whiskey's effect on our brains. Salah and I stare at each other for a long time, in a sort of reciprocal accommodation, in search of a bit of lucidity. When we bring our eyes to hers, we realize that the latter are starting to break through now. As the fog that leads them astray lifts, they regain their mobility and move about slowly: onto the ceiling, the wall, the fireplace, the fire, the portrait of Dalila leaning against the wall. As her eyes meet it, a slight smile relaxes her lips. We hardly dare breathe. Then, looking again at the fire, and after a moment of meditation, she begins murmuring. We crowd around her.

'He'd bought pomegranates for me. The pomegranate, the most beautiful of fruits, the most regal. A doll's crown on an old gold-colored piece of leather, spattered with scarlet. And when you break it open, a honeycombed heart where each drop of blood is set in a diamond skin and encloses in its breast an opal shaving. And when you bite into it, this mixture of liquid and filaments that leaves a taste of the forbidden in your mouth.

'He'd bought me pomegranates.

'He would wear his Tuareg saroual and his big Rif-style hat that I liked.[1] A hat whose reverse side, made of cloth, laughed with the colors of green, orange, red, yellow, and purple, like a celebration dancing in a circle around his head. He'd begun to juggle with pomegranates. I'd try to imitate him. He'd laugh. I'd laugh. My mother came in.'

'Where were you?'

'She went by without answering. He gave me the pomegranates that he had in his hand and he followed her.'

'Where were you?'

'She would say nothing. She'd busy herself.'

'Where were you?'

'He kept raising his voice until he was screaming.'

'Where were you? Where were you?'

'Infuriated, she turned toward him and said, "Now what did they tell you? Don't you understand they're trying to poison your life? Which neighbor was I with this time?" '

'He jumped on her. They fought. Punches, claws, cries of rage . . . All of a sudden, my mother fell, her head on the millstone. She wasn't moving anymore. He collapsed onto her: "Aïcha! Aïcha! Aïcha!" '

'My mother no longer answered. Time had stopped in her eyes. From now on a rupture separated her from us. I cried out, "Oummi! Oummi!"[2]

'He was looking at her, then looking at me silently, and his eyes said to me, "I didn't mean to! I didn't mean to! I didn't mean to!" He was looking at her in silence and his eyes were weeping. I stopped crying out. Two drops of water dripped from the bucket hung on the pulley and plunged into the bottom of the well, one after the other.

---

1. *Saroual:* loose-fitting cloth pants worn in the southern regions of North Africa. Rif: a mountain range in northern Morocco inhabited by sedentary farmers.

2. *Oummi:* mama.

'He got up. He stared at us again, my mother, stretched out, and me, gripping her, and then he went out. I never saw him again.

'My little three-year-old sister, who was ill, was in bed in a corner of the room. My uncle and the neighbors buried her two days after my mother. I was five years old.

'In the ksar it was rumored that we were a cursed family. For a long time I was convinced of it. When I'd walk down the street, children would run away from me as I approached. Hopping frogs scattered in panic. To escape from this, I got myself a bell: for a few days I dragged an empty can, attached to a string, behind me. Then my eyes withdrew from everything. I withdrew myself from present time.

'In order not to be completely alone, I dreamed about my other self that had left with him. I saw them, very far away, on the other side of the world, in a northern desert where no one could ever find them again. He was juggling snowballs. The snow was falling apart in the air and falling down again on his laughter, in a crystal rain. She was dancing, making her big Rif-style hat twirl around. They were going from village to village like circus entertainers, people living from celebration. The books that told about snow and biting cold placed gentle murmurs in my silence. Ice crystals circulated in my blood and gave me shivers in the midst of torpor.

'The other part of me, the part who had disappeared with my mother and my sister, I couldn't picture her. I had banished her. Or maybe it was she who didn't want me. I don't know. Yet I always felt her in my shadow, a silent noise attached to my thoughts and whose invisible thread I didn't succeed in cutting.

'Within two days, all of them abandoned me. I grew up alone, anorexic and hounded, with the soul of a tragic traveling performer. I never ate a pomegranate again. I didn't eat anything anymore, I didn't move anymore, except by virtue of a last-minute self who persisted in breathing, sleeping, walking, a sleepwalker caught in the inextricable entanglement of solitude and hatred.'

'You should never have returned here! You should never have!' says Salah.

[131]

'Yes, I should have. For the last few years, all that remains to me of my parents are outlines, faceless ghosts. I have no photo, neither of one nor the other. Yet another piece of myself that repudiates and abandons me. And then, of the people from here, I remembered only sniggering, insinuations, and insults behind my back. Returning to practice here lets me replenish the supply of their pain, their complaints, and their moaning, the abyss of their sadness, their wounded looks; it lets me give reality to their flesh again, to approach them in their totality, neither entirely good nor completely bad, but conservative and backward. That saves me from black-and-white judgments, exorcises perverted grudges, even if I realize that my memories still weigh on me, and always more than the burdens of their memory.'

'Insults, you said?' I asked.

'Yes, insults and fears. Insults because of the fear I inspired. As a child, I looked at people without seeing them. I walked all day long to exhaust my terrified feelings. The only landmarks I had were the odors of different places. My sense of smell was the guide of my blindness. From time to time I'd become aware that my behavior was out of the bounds of what was considered normal. But too much emptiness in myself prevented me from anchoring myself in what was customary. If I'd been treated as a crazy woman, that wouldn't have shocked me in the least. I never felt very far from insanity; the absurd seemed to me the best retort to monstrosity. But no! At first they said, "Cursed whore's daughter, cursed daughter of the cursed." But I quickly realized that I was powerfully protected by the cover of my supposed damnation. For a long time the words "cursed one" protected me from being showered with rocks and other forms of aggression that the word "whore" could have brought upon me. I cultivated my curses as shields, but also as eccentricities, and in order to provoke. I never had the soul of one defeated.

'When I reached secondary school, a new French doctor arrived in the village. He took complete charge of me to save me from my isolation. That's when the word "whore," blown out of proportion by false rumors, lit up by even more vivid memories of the torments of war, covered over

the word "cursed." I become the roumi's whore. In the streets I was ac-
cused of "giving to the roumis," of consuming pork and alcohol in their
home. I was a virgin, and I would remain so for a long time, for lack of interest rather than because of chastity. I only tasted alcohol at the university, and as for eating pork . . . These words sullied the few feelings of
affection that I had. Paul and Jeanne Challes had the worst problems because of me. I gritted my teeth and told myself: they won't have my head
like they had my mother's. At the end of two years, the situation was such
that the Challeses' contracts were terminated. They were expelled from
the region. My uncle had just died. Thanks to the help of understanding
and influential people, Paul Challes was able to get a place for me as a
boarder in a high school in Oran.

'If Algeria had really been committed to the path of progress, if its
leaders had really worked at making mentalities evolve, I would have no
doubt recovered. I would have forgotten bit by bit. But the country's current events and the fate of women here constantly plunge me back into
my past dramas, link me to all those women who are tyrannized. The per-
secutions and the humiliations endured by them reach me and reopen
my wounds. Distance attenuates nothing. Pain is the strongest bond between humans. Stronger than all resentments.'

A sob reminds us of Alilou's presence. As evidenced by her surprise,
Sultana seems to discover him. Salah moves his hand onto the child's
head: 'Meet Alilou, king of the ruins.'

'Why did you go to the ksar at night?' I asked her.

'I left Aïn Nekhla by car. Then I got off the road and drove toward the
sand wind. When I reached it, I stopped the car. There were two headlights in front of me, the big-engined car's. Afterward . . .'

She looks at me worriedly before concluding, 'Afterward, I can't remember very well.'

'Sultana, there wasn't any sand wind today,' I say softly to her.

'So I'm talking complete nonsense?'

'You're too tired, too stirred up by all of this. Anyone would be for
much less.'

Panic takes over her eyes. She looks alternatively at each of us, Salah and me. Salah takes her hand. I caress her hair. She calms down bit by bit.

'Sultana, you must leave here. Last night some vandals broke the kitchen windowpanes. You can't stay here at the mercy of these people. Come with me to Algiers or go instead to Oran if you prefer.'

She reflects and seems to be struggling with herself for a long time before murmuring, 'I have to return to Montpellier. A few days should suffice for me to make arrangements, find another person to replace me, in view of a longer absence. I hope that this break will allow me better judgment. Undoubtedly, I should return. If not, how will I escape from the anxiety of leaving without relief, of wandering without ever arriving, of the loss of faces that riddle and burn my memory, of the tyranny of a country that has always bartered my affections and my loves, for terrors or remorse, that has always condemned all my hopes, that locks effort in solitude, that transforms success into distress? How do you cure yourself of anguish about anguish, of its hypnotic power and its aphasia? From this return, I can only bring back masses of fallen rocks revived in my mind. I no longer want to endure the unlivable, nostalgia with no way out. But I'll calmly reconsider all of that in Montpellier. I'll keep you posted.'

'Return to cross the desert with me. We'll stay there until you've had your fill. Then we'll leave by boat. I'll take you to the Kerkennah Islands. You'll see, it's a bit of the desert in the sea, an orange water lily dancing on the water.'

Salah transfixes me with a murderous look. With a smile fixed on her face, Sultana looks at both of us for a long time. Suddenly, she bursts into sobs. She cries as one cries for joy, with a radiant face.

9

SULTANA

Last night I wept. It's the first thought that comes to me, as soon as I open my eyes. It fills me with happiness. How, why, all of a sudden did a chance hiccup tap a reserve of tears? In what lost country? I sank into sleep, relieved. Unaware of anything. I didn't even dream of Yacine.

Was it Ali Marbah following me in his car? With a vehicle other than his own? Or is my imagination completely out of control, summoning a sand wind that blows only in me? I know it's capable of everything. Doesn't it bring the dead back to life? What does it matter? This morning, I'm not in the mood to abandon myself to either melancholy or worry. I stretch voluptuously. Then I push back the blanket and sit up on the sofa. I discover Salah, Vincent, and little Alilou stretched out on mattresses on the floor. In a sort of fulfilled dizzy spell I tremble with emotion at seeing them there. Huddled around me in my sleep, this variety of males is an invaluable gift. I get up on the tips of my toes, light, given wings by gratitude.

I take a shower and take particular care to make myself beautiful again. A bit of makeup on the dark rings under my eyes makes my suntan stand out. A brilliant coral color on my lips, my curls brushed, given more body . . . but above all, it's this gleam that my eyes have found again, something between insolence and challenge that illuminates me and cheers me up this morning. I look at myself, gaze into my eyes. I recognize my rebelliousness in the light in those eyes of mine. I scrutinize it, bombard it with questions:

[135]

So my metamorphosis this morning is your work? In any case, the sign of your return. I should have suspected it! What made you change your mind? These libations of tears, a drunkenness till now unknown? The emotion due to the presence of two men to love, the stirrings of desire and my weakness that never knows how to choose anything except flight? There! You're gloating, I know! The fear of dying of boredom or hunger far away from me? The plan to return to Montpellier? Are you just the Western woman in me? No, I don't think so. You're duality itself, and you never worry about your source of satisfaction at any given moment. Because for you everything is ephemeral and worry doesn't seem to touch you except to mark the hollow from which the caustic laughter of your derision spurts in a rush.

A flower of disdain tacked onto her smile and a side glance, she stares at me, contemplates me in scattered pieces on the chessboard of her will.

Strengthened by the feeling of my recomposed complexity, I leave the bathroom. I make coffee. While it's running through the filter, I get dressed. I choose an orange dress whose cheeriness I like. Back in the kitchen I discover the broken windowpanes. I'll have to ask Khaled if there's a glazier in Aïn Nekhla. I'll have to tell Halima to come back to do the housework and to cook up some genuine local dishes. I'll have to call Air Algeria to reserve my seats. Probably for next week. I'll have to let the appropriate person know about this departure.

Montpellier: Return or not? For a trip or for someone to replace me? Salah or Vincent? When one has always acted under constraint or with urgency, having a choice all of a sudden is frightening, a booby-trapped luxury that you stare at as you're backing away from it.

When I left Montpellier the elm trees were shedding their leaves. For a long time the vines have been a blood color as the foliage of these trees turns up its nose at autumn's flamboyant attacks. But with an end-of-November burst of north wind, they abruptly let go all their old castoffs, which then yellow at their feet.

At home I have to trim the hedge, add a bit of peat moss to the hydrangeas and camellias, cover the roots of the bougainvillea and the

[136]

plumbago with straw before it freezes . . . I have to . . . In vain this interior gardening clears away the underbrush of my confusion; all the same, it's troubling to feel like I'm here and there at the same time, the other one and this one.

In the refrigerator I find butter that Salah must have brought from Algiers. I settle in and have breakfast with a good appetite. Salah and Vincent get up at the same time. They greet me simultaneously with a delighted whistle. Their lingering eyes breathe a revival of pleasure into me. Their verbal sparring matches, their play at rivalry delight and move me. But how . . . how can I make them understand my terror of choice, of settling down? How can I make them understand that my survival is only in moving around, migrating? When you're in this state, with burning eagerness in your heart, projection into the future is almost impossible. The emptiness that you drag around inside of you, composed of skin, claws, eyes, nerves, in total collapse or on alert, is always too intense to be tolerated for very long; too busy gorging itself on the present to envision itself sharing or partaking of the future. My return here will have at least served that purpose, to destroy my last illusions of being anchored. How can I persuade them of that when I myself took so many years to admit it?

Alilou, whose little fennec's nose peeps out from beneath the bushy hair that conceals his eyes, saves me from their questions.

Someone knocks violently at the door. Salah puts down his coffee and leaves to open it.

'What are *you* doing here again?'

'And her, where is she?'

Bakkar, the mayor, is accompanied by Ali Marbah and by a third thief with the same insane look.

'We don't want you staying here anymore! Aïn Nekhla isn't a whorehouse! You even sleep with foreigners! Two men at the same time! We know you! You're still a danger to girls, the village's sin,' he yells, losing his fetid chewing tobacco in sputters, as soon as he sees me.

[137]

Vincent's face is consternation itself. As for Salah, he violently slams the door in their faces. He turns to us and declares, 'You have to let fanatic hatred and stupidity consume themselves.'

Taken over by hysteria, the men frenetically pound on the door, pour out threats, promise me capital sentences by a 'court of believers.'

'Do you still want to return here?' worries Salah.

'Yes, but not at just any price. I'd like to return for the Dalilas and the Alilous, on a mission for the eyes of children who mustn't be abandoned to distress or contamination. I'd like to return for the desert. But what's the desert good for? Have I really admired it since my return? If I feel like a shadow far from the desert, it is only a dusty ghost, confined by the wounds of what I see when I'm here. You believe you're returning and it's a foreigner in you who discovers and is surprised. You don't even find yourself in what this foreigner sees. The words of these men and the evils of the village destroy the scenery. I'll see this from Montpellier, from the perspective of another, more distant and wise self.'

A crowd of men surround the hospital. Alilou, who has been at my heels since he awoke, bravely takes my hand. I squeeze his tightly. I don't look at anyone. We cut through the crowd.

'Slut!' yells out a voice that I believe to be Ali Marbah's.

'Shut your mouth, queer!' orders an anonymous person.

Alilou is jolted. I feel it through his little hand. I turn around. My eyes instantly find Ali Marbah's. Anger makes me bristle.

'You're just a bunch of frustrated people, in your head and your underpants! You've never had any brains. You're just erect penises! An unsatisfied erection. Your eyes are nothing but vermin. Vermin that constantly dirty, gnaw at, and devour women!'

I turned my words loose with delight. Taken over by the wildness of his nervous tics, Ali Marbah's eyes squint, roll, and threaten. Deep silence falls on the men, increases the tension. I push back the laughter rising in me. I shrug my shoulders, face them casually and mockingly, and con-

[138]

tinue on my way. In front of me a rock smashes into the hospital door. 'Son of a whore!' someone yells.

I climb the steps and slam the heavy door behind me. Khaled immediately greets me.

'Come, come!'

He pushes Alilou and me into the office and closes the door.

'The mayor just came by here as mad as a hornet when it's just beginning to get warm. He chased the men out of the waiting room: "You mustn't wait for her. Leave, leave! We don't want her here anymore! She doesn't deserve to have this job!" He didn't know what he looked like, he who treats people like cattle. He didn't like Yacine either. But he was never brave enough to come and cross swords with him. He went about doing his dirty work, the bastard. Most of the women, their backs up against his outrageous behavior, refused to leave the place. I didn't have time to react when they rose up and barred his passage to the hallway. "We're going to squish you, flea of our misery!" one of them screamed.

'He backed up.

' "We're going to make you drink all of your arrogance," cried out another woman.

'They were moving forward one step. He was backing up two. They were seething with rage. Suddenly, he was pale and mute under the assault of their sarcasm.

' "What do you want with Sultana Medjahed?"

' "To make her suffer the same fate as her mother?"

' "You know you'll never be able to do that because Sultana is a free woman, she is! Is that what enrages you? In spite of all the tyranny and discrimination they endure, there are after all some free Algerian women! Oh, oh, that bothers you and makes you feel like you don't have a dick anymore!"

' "That made you crazy not to have had her mother, huh? You never could swallow the fact that she preferred a foreigner to you."

[139]

' "Do you think we've forgotten that it was your mouth of a goat in heat that started off and kept up the malicious gossip, to the point of drama?"

' "So martyring and throwing into the street your own women will never be enough for you? You still have to ogle the neighbors' women and expect to control those women who are infinitely out of your reach?'

' "And your accomplice, that demon Ali Marbah. Tell him I'll slice his skin up, from top to toe, everywhere, especially down below, there where he's got the devil's fire. Tell him that afterward I'll sprinkle him with salt and pepper and I'll throw him to the sun and the wind, to the vultures for them to peck at his wounds. You know, you do, that he let my daughter die! After she gave birth, she lost all her blood. 'Take her to the hospital, ask the doctor to come!' we women said. 'I'm sick of her only giving me daughters! So let her bleed out this tainted blood! That'll put her mess inside back together,' said that scum."

' "As soon as it was daybreak we sent a child in secret to summon the doctor. But it was too late. She'd emptied herself during the night while he was snoring. Tell him I'll drink his blood all the way to the last drop."

'It's Lalla Fatima who poured out these threats against Marbah. Before, Lalla Fatima was a gentle and self-effacing woman. Since the loss of her only daughter we don't recognize her anymore. One day when I was giving her a shot in the infirmary, she grabbed a pencil left lying on the counter. She took a sharpened knife out of the pocket of her saroual and in a rage started to gash the pencil. "Most of our men are like this toward their wives: black inside with wood around them. We have to cut them like this until we're finished!" When there was nothing left of the pencil, she stared at the blackened knife blade with as much disgust as if she'd been spattered with blood. "Give me some alcohol," she murmured. She cleaned off the knife before putting it back in her pocket. Silent and furious, she left me.'

'And what'd Bakkar say?'

'Nothing, nothing. Fear and astonishment made him swallow his tongue. In backing up in the hallway, he ended up banging into the front door. He opened it and took off amid their laughter and mockery. I couldn't believe my eyes.'

'Those people are so afraid of women! They're so sick about them."'

I open the waiting room door. There are a dozen women with the learned expression of those holding a war council. One of the oldest women gets up when I appear. My mother would have been her age. Long, wizened, sculptured, wearing the black melehfa of the Doui-Miniî, my mother's tribe.[1]

'We know who you are, my daughter. We're pleased that Sultana Medjahed became a beautiful woman and, in addition, a doctor. We mustn't give in to these tyrants! We women need you. Until now there've only been male doctors here. You, you're one of us. You can understand us. The schoolteacher and the midwife came a little while ago, just to give you their support. They weren't able to stay longer because of their work. But they asked us to tell you. Thirty years of putting up with party members is enough suffering. We don't want to fall under an even more ruthless yoke, that of the fundamentalists. What do these forgers of faith think? Are they all prophets of a new Allah that we might not have been aware of until now? Heretics, that's what they are. Their words and their very existence are insults to the memory of our forefathers, our religion, and our history. I'm a former resistance fighter speaking to you. A woman who doesn't understand by what perversion our country's independence deprived us of our dignity and our rights, when we fought for it.

'We're with you. We passed the word around for all of us together to come and see you today. Join us! We're asking you to care for us. All of us will wait here until you've finished. The schoolteacher and the midwife will come and join us. Then we'll cross the village in a group to go to Khaled's. His wife is making us couscous. We have to talk, give each other a little solidarity. They have to know that we won't let them push us around anymore. That we're even ready to take up arms again if we have

---

1. *Melehfa:* a kind of sari, usually black.

to. My daughter, *one hand alone cannot applaud.* Before, the widow and the woman spurned by her husband were taken back by their tribe. There they were fed and protected. If they had no liberty, at least they didn't have to worry about anything. In times past, the old woman ruled over a large family. She had the power of her sons who had become men. Her wealth was the respect of her sons. She enjoyed all joys, all of the honors earned and saved up during the difficult years of her youth.'

She catches her breath, passes her hand under her grin, rubs her hand against the cloth of her melehfa. The women behind her are a wall of silence, cemented together in unity. 'Speechless and full of fury,' Khaled said about one of them. I find them all to be thus, speechless and full of fury. So beautiful in their fury. Between them and me is Alilou and the black stars of his eyes. Eyes of an adult childhood, the grown-ups' worst condemnation. The old woman begins speaking again: 'Now the tribes have fragmented, some in the Tell, others abroad. Now modern houses may be comfortable, but they are lacking in generosity. Modernity? It displays its superficiality to our eyes and its doors close on a small number of people. Reducing the family to a man, a woman, and their children conveys exclusion to the other members of the tribe. Now the attraction of cities has torn apart the clans. Now the length of absence from the family has ended what were already loose ties, has demolished solidarity. Now the widow and the spurned woman find themselves in the street with a swarm of children. No one can feed them any longer or protect them. No one. We've always taught women that the street was not their territory, that they only had to take care of their domestic life, and now each day a growing number of them, mop in hand, slaves to more and more arrogance, have to confront the garbage of all the bureaucracies, all the institutions and laws that abuse them. Now a woman gets nothing from all the work and the humiliations and scoldings she's subjected to. All the will and abnegation she can give to her younger days no longer serve her in any way. When she becomes old, her daughters-in-law no longer want her, her children are scattered. She crowds in with the most generous of her children, if there is a generous one. What sadness to real-

[142]

ize that her life has only been slavery and humiliation in a continual state of powerlessness! So how do we carry on a tradition that no one respects any longer? How can we perpetuate a way of living that doesn't accord to us any more consideration, at any moment of our life? We must speak. We must give ourselves solidarity. *One hand alone cannot applaud,* and we can't take anymore! We are so worn out.'

Other speeches, other acknowledgments of failure. I advise. I acquiesce or comfort. Then, wearied by so much confusion, I take refuge in the office. With their veil, they put down their rebellion, their demands, the fire in their eyes.

In front of the doctor, they're nothing more than a moaning or stammering koulchite. I scrutinize koulchites. Jumbled koulchites, bits of suffering, piled up in an inextricable tangle. I try to find their ends. I spread open, I untangle, I sort. I get discouraged. My exasperation grates between time's pincers, and clumsiness lies in wait for me. I'm not a psychoanalyst, and here in the south of souths, the doctor is deprived of even the most vital drugs.

Loss of meaning is a koulchite in preparation, a nucleus of distress in each cell of the body of fate.

A few men returned to me. 'They don't run us, they don't, those dogs,' thunders forth one of them.

'We don't have anything against you, we don't. You're not a woman. You're a doctor,' another judges.

'I'm a woman doctor! A woman before anything, do you hear me? And I have no need of the bragging of some, of the decrepit and bombastic morality, or of the cowardice of others!'

'Madam, don't say we're cowards,' a mountain of a man beseeches me, with a martyr's groanings. 'We're ready to fight them to defend you.'

'Big deal! Start by defending yourselves against this fundamentalist scum! As for myself, your stupidity armed me a long time ago!'

Vexed mumbling.

[143]

'Even going to the marabout or the doctor is now a sin? Where are we headed? "They" need only tell us clearly: lie down on the ground and let yourselves die!' a third person says indignantly.

At midday a veritable delegation leaves the hospital. Nothing's missing except banners and flags. Slogans pound in people's heads. Khaled and three other strong men are at the rear. Khaled's wife, Zyneb, greets us. Around platters of couscous, koulchites set aside, the conversations explode more than ever. Some of the women possess indisputable talents as actors and mimes. They make fun of their ills and their misery, and their eyes brim over with malicious tears. They deride stereotyped formal language and the official saber rattling, and their looks are like daggers. They denounce the venomous zeal of the Islamists and the pupils of their eyes flame up like firebrands. They inveigh against the spinelessness and the simian behavior of women who've converted to using the hijab, and bitterness distorts all their features.[1]

'As for me, I'm going to tell you, my mind was a lot more composed when I went regularly to the hadras.[2] Being in a trance was an effective antidote for me,' affirms an ancient woman, her hair red with henna.

'Why not organize one at one or another's house?' a pregnant young woman with an enormous belly asks.

'These last years we've lost everything, even those moments of healthy release, and we've lost ourselves,' another woman argues, wearing heavy African jewelry.

'As for me, I've neither a husband nor a grown son. So come to my place Friday afternoon. We'll have cakes and tea.'

The latter will experience for certain, I know, some remissions of their koulchites, I think. When the trays of tea arrive, the former resistance fighter asks for silence and brings up her project for partnership. They become solemn. Little by little I realize that there is no improvisation

1. *Hijab:* curtain, protection, veil.
2. *Hadras:* meeting of women where singing is accompanied by a trance state.

going on here: I am in the process of witnessing a planned and prepared meeting. Thus my presence in the village has only expedited what was already brewing.

The afternoon is well on its way when they decide that they have advanced sufficiently to have a first meeting. Objectives have been set, tasks handed out.

'Are you with us for sure? You're not abandoning us?' worries the Doui-Minii's leader. 'We want you to be our president. But you'll have to be more discreet with your friends!'

'More discreet means no longer having them over at all, right?'

I can't help laughing my head off. Their sudden tensing is such obvious proof of their common outlook and, as an indirect result, my isolation. Disillusioned, I shrug my shoulders.

'Do like us. We watch our steps here. For treats we go to Oran or to Algiers,' the schoolteacher shares with me, on the side, in French.

I stare around the room at them.

'No, no, I won't be your president. The schoolteacher is much more appropriate for that than I am. Maybe you need the doctor, but the woman . . .'

'But you're also from here!'

'Will I still be one of you when I tell you that I don't want to renounce anything? And anyway, what does it mean to be one of you? To have had neither a tribe nor a family to save me from nothing but the sharing of habit and conventions, from their constraints and their contradictions. Rebellion against injustice is one thing, the true desire for liberty is another, which demands a much larger step, sometimes some changes.'

Impassive faces. It's not worth continuing. Uneasiness separates us for a moment. Then one of them says to me, 'I remember so well the day that you left the village.'

'Me, too!'

The woman is not aware of my irony and continues. 'This doctor had come looking for you. He'd parked his car on the square of the ksar. You were seen coming out of the cul de sac. He was carrying your suitcase.

Your eyes were terrible, terrible. Women, children, and men began following you. There was a great silence. Before getting into the car, you turned around and ran your eyes over all of us. And then you stared at Bakkar and you said in a harsh voice, "You and your band, you're the rot of this country. But I'm going to study, and I'll be stronger than all of your cowardly and disgraceful acts. Look hard at me. I don't give a damn about you! And I'll come back one day to tell you so." Yes, you said that, and you even repeated, "I don't give a damn about you!" Then you got into the car and you both left.'

Another woman interrupts her. 'Then another woman lets out from underneath her veil, "There's no doubt about it, that little one is courageous!" '

'Oh, yeah? I thought my condemnation was unanimous. I thought I was forbidden in the village. In any case, all I heard raining down on me was "Whore!" At the present time, at least, some disagreements and confrontations exist between people. The unanimities of times past, especially concerning banishment, alarmed me. They served me. I'm always suspicious of the dangers of consensus!'

'We didn't approve of all the reprobation that fell on you. But we had no means, no influence, to intervene in your favor.'

'Uh-huh, and you've acquired this power that you were missing?'

'When you're backed into a corner, you're forced to counterattack. Maybe that's where our strength will come from. They can enslave us or break us one by one. They'll think twice about it if we unite.'

There's an awkward silence. Then, all smiles, one of them murmurs, 'I remember your mother so well! She was so beautiful, much more beautiful than even you.'

'Yes?'

The embarrassment fades. The faces smile. Another woman continues, 'She was beautiful and cheerful. That's why she died young. Life here doesn't tolerate cheerfulness, especially in a woman.'

And another woman says, 'And she knew she was beautiful. She liked looking at herself. She liked to make herself even more beautiful, and here, that's already The Sin.'

And another woman, 'And me, I remember your father so well. A big Chaâmbi with a mustache like only the Chaâmbis have, and with their grandeur.'[1]

I cry out, 'Yes! Yes!'

Their faces become tender. A sound like a radiant flute rises in me. A joy that spreads, reaching all of my silent corners. And another: 'And he, so handsome with his pride and his Chaâmbi mustache, he, the foreigner, arrived and took the most beautiful woman here, the one promised to Bakkar.'

And another: 'Bakkar went crazy over it and so did the members of his tribe, the Ouled Gerrir, with him. Your mother's tribe, the Doui-Miniî, laughed up their sleeves and drank in this joke like fresh buttermilk.'

'The rivalry between the two tribes is legendary. They never take sides, the better to tear each other apart later on.'

'It's always dangerous for a foreigner to be caught in the confrontation between two enemy tribes. Besides, it's always a drama to be a foreigner somewhere.'

I say, 'No, it's not a drama to be a foreigner! No! It's a tormented richness. It's a wrenching intoxicated by discovery and freedom and which cannot be prevented from cultivating its losses.'

These words find no echo in them. One of the women starts up again. 'And the Chaâmbi loved his wife. He loved his wife so much that for the others, it was another sin.'

'Really, he loved my mother that much?'

'Yes, yes, he loved her, the big Chaâmbi, as a man, losing himself, can love a girl.'

'Really, that much?' I asked again.

My voice is trembling. My fingers are trembling. I am a flute drunken with the wind. Another adds: 'This great happiness, perceived as some-

---

1. Chaâmbi: from the Chaâmba tribe (high plateaus of Méchéria), known for its gallant riders and its resistance to colonization.

[147]

thing out of the ordinary, stirred up jealousy, let loose tongues, and armed accusations of sorcery. So inevitably, misfortune occurred.'

'Yes, inevitably, a great misfortune! And also, your father loved you way too much,' one woman exclaimed, her crescent-shaped smile against the insult of her tattoo.

'It was that obvious? You can never love your daughter too much!'

'He loved you too much,' she concluded, her tattoos knotted together. 'If he'd loved you less, if he'd considered you only as his daughter, you would have lived among us. But because he loved you too much, he made you rebellious and difficult, blind to our expectations and even to the attention we paid you. It was as if you'd come from elsewhere, with customs from elsewhere. And misfortune made you even more foreign. So you also left.'

'That's the drama! This total rejection that crushes you and excludes you from everything. A first exile from childhood that leaves you with nothing more than the exquisite wound of lucidity. Later, conditioned by uncertainty and solitude, you're nothing more than a desire without a possible hitch, put into orbit around fears, an unending flight.'

Disconcerted, they look at me. They, unified by the same stupor. I, once again so alone. 'You speak like a book!' Salah's retort rings in my head. What good are words lost in incomprehension. I laugh and make them anxious. The expressions of their eyes can't be put into words. Yet I know, I feel, their genuine desire to 'buy me back,' to link me to them. I'm not insensitive to that.

One of them interrupts the silence in a light voice. 'He took you with him everywhere. He carried you around on his shoulders, your legs around his neck. And everyone said to him, "Chaâmbi, you don't carry around a girl that way! Chaâmbi, put her down, she's only a girl!" He laughed with his strong laugh and retorted, "You bunch of ignoramuses, look carefully at my daughter, she's worth more than all of your sons combined!"'

'He'd say that? I no longer remember.'

'You were too young,' exclaims the ancient one, her hair red with henna.

And another one continued: 'He'd say that with his strong laugh. And everybody knew that, on his part, it wasn't only a joke. The proof is that he put you in school when no other girl from the ksar had set foot there yet. Your father was the foreigner from here. An educated foreigner, different from us.'

School, the first rupture . . . He read books by the light of the oil lamp. He told me stories about snow, wind, and white wolves in the countries where it was cold. Stories like a great calmness, a shimmering sleep.

They're all quiet and they look at me. My head is full of one image. An image without words and the soft caress of the flute's wind.

'Have you seen your father again?' asks the woman who had talked for so long.

'No, never.'

'How unfortunate!' says another.

'They say he may have gone abroad,' ventures another.

'Maybe in a desert of snow?' I suggest.

'Others say he may have joined the resistance and that he met his death there,' murmurs a member of the Ouled Gerrir tribe.

And another: 'What's certain is that he must have died. If he hadn't, you would have heard from him. He would have asked you to come and be with him.'

'Yes, that's for certain,' confirms another.

They continue to go on about it, but in my head their voices become distant. Then I see him again. I see him, he, my first instance of being torn away, my first suffering. I see him with his Chaâmbi-style mustache, with his eyes, two mouthfuls of night, saturated with stars. I see him, the foreigner from here. I see him, the laughing stranger, in the northern steppes, in the iridescent atmosphere of his readings. I see him walking in the four seasons of those steppes. In their virginal snow. In their blizzard, like a story unleashed. In their playful spring, drunken with its orgies. I see him, contemplative, near a spring where hordes of birds drink, their wings heavy from their return flight and already trembling at departure's call. I see him, unrepentant watcher of the absolute, taster of differences, in the fullness of autumn, in its peaceful redness. Then again in the white and cutting laughter of winter. I see, in the night of his eyes, the desert's fire. I see him with the multiple eyes of absence, the eyes of deprivation. I see him in the moments' farandoles once again looped together outside of oblivion.

'Your mother was one of us, of the Doui-Miniî, emancipated slaves, taken from the heart of Africa,' says the old resistance fighter.

'Yes, I know.'

And my mother also rises in me again. She overflows my heart and my eyes, washes entirely over me. I float in her. My mother, river of tears, in the twists and turns of my inmost depths, the inaudible trembling of my doubts. My mother, flood of emptiness, cruel silence that drowns the stridency of the day.

In the late afternoon Vincent and I transport Yacine's paintings to Khaled's. I will feel calmer knowing that they're there. I want to give Dalila's portrait and the drawing and painting materials to her.

In Tammar we go first to the bookstore. Vincent is eager to give the little girl some dictionaries and a few books. Then he leaves me in front of her house. At the door, Dalila greets me. She quickly overcomes her surprise so as to order me: 'Don't talk about Samia!'

I don't have time to respond; her mother is standing before me. I explain to her who I am and that I've organized a drawing contest in the schools.

'Dalila is the most gifted of all the students. She earned first prize. I was eager to bring it to her myself here at her home, to convince her parents of the importance of her gifts. She's done well, very, very well!'

'The only good that a daughter must have in her head is obedience to her parents and their blessing,' retorts her mother, clearly embarrassed by my presence and by the materials and books unwrapped before her eyes.

'She absolutely must continue on this path. To encourage her, I did her portrait. Look.'

As I uncover the painting, I see Dalila's stupefaction in her dropped jaw. Mouth open, she doesn't say a word. Her mother looks at the portrait for a long time. She ends up conceding, 'You draw well too.'

She gets up stiffly, grabs the painting, and hides it in the only wardrobe in the room, under a pile of linen. She says to me, as she puts back the key in a belt pocket, 'I'll leave you with Dalila. I'm going to prepare some tea.'

Dalila immediately recovers her spirits. 'She's reserved. Very, very reserved, but cornered by silence.'

'That's the least one can say.'

'In any case, she can't yell at me. She can't say anything to me. You lie almost as well as I do. That reassures me about you. You're still Algerian in the way you lie. With the way you are, so far away, so honest about your truths, which shock the people from here, I thought you'd forgotten what girls do to trick the others.'

She strokes a tube of paint while looking intently at the wardrobe. 'It's funny to think of this Dalila with linen over her face like a woman with a chador.[1] Don't you think the moths are going to eat out her eyes?' And without waiting for my response: 'I'm going to buy some camphor and put it on the painting's eyes. That Dalila is going to sleep until I'll be able to live.' Then, pointing to the books and the drawing paraphernalia: 'Those things seem foreign in the middle of utensils just for eating and drinking. You'd think they were trabendo merchandise. I'll take all of that over to Ouarda's or else my brothers will trade them for hashish or American cigarettes.'

'Why mustn't we speak about Samia?' I ask, suddenly remembering her plea.

'Because!'

'If you don't tell me why, I'll ask your mother some questions about her.'

---

1. Chador: a large square cloth worn by women to cover the head and face.

[151]

'No, no! Don't do that! Samia . . . doesn't exist.'

'What do you mean, she doesn't exist?'

'Samia's just a sister eyeballed in my dreams. It's just that all the girls who leave Algeria, people talk about them so much that they come into my dreams. Now it's as if it were a little bit you.'

'Really? And the other one, the one who leaves no footprints on the dune?'

'I won't tell you that, even if you repeat it to my mother. I don't care!'

'Don't worry. I won't say anything about it.'

Pensive, she contemplates her treasure for a long time before confiding to me, 'You know, the people here, they're so poor that they never keep three cents to enjoy themselves. They only keep them for burials and catastrophes. Girls do the same with dreams and lies. They're for nothing except to repair life's holes.'

Then leaving her seriousness behind for a little mischievousness: 'With you and me, it's not a drawing contest, it's a lying contest! . . . Ah, ah, all the drawings filled with nastiness that I'm going to do!'

The night is somber and heavy. Myriads of stars form constellations in the sky. With no surprises, the road goes by in the straight trench formed by the headlights. In the back seat, his head thrown back, Salah is singing. A magnificent and poignant Andalusian song. At the wheel, Vincent seems calm and focused on this song. My forehead against the pane, I scrutinize the sky.

'In no other place do you see as many stars,' I murmur.

Vincent drives slowly. I let myself be rocked by Salah's recital. I think we're all happy to be here together. We did some errands. At the market in Tammar there were truffles for a laughable price.

'They're not the same ones we have at home,' a scrupulous merchant warned Vincent. This evening we've agreed to prepare for ourselves a feast fit for a king, to share some good wine, and to hell with our anxieties and worries.

'Oh, look at that glow rising from Aïn Nekhla!' exclaims Vincent.

Salah becomes silent and leans against my seat. 'Something out of the ordinary is going on, is there a fire?'

I stiffen, suddenly full of anxiety. Vincent speeds up.

'It's a fire for sure!' declares Salah.

We stay quiet until we reach Aïn Nekhla.

A hullabaloo reigns in the village. People are running in every direction, calling out to each other. Vincent suddenly brakes. Before us, Yacine's house is nothing more than flames.

'The paintings!' screams Salah, rushing out of the car.

I hold him back by his arm. 'Don't move. They're in a safe place.'

'Where? How?'

'We moved them to Khaled's.'

He collapses on the back seat and lets out a big sigh of relief. I discover another center of fire. 'It's burning over there, too.'

'That's city hall,' declares Salah.

An explosion drowns out the grumbling. Khaled and four children, one of them Alilou, burst out of the night.

'Don't stay here, it's dangerous! Marbah and his band burned down the doctor's house. The women, informed by the children, set city hall on fire. There's a monstrous fight going on in the center of the village. People are saying two men have died. I'm afraid there'll be other victims.'

'We have to go see if there are any wounded people,' says Salah.

Again I hold him back.

'No, we'll be such beautiful targets. Don't forget that we're the ones who touched off the crisis. I was afraid the house might be ransacked. But I didn't think they'd go so far as to burn it. Fortunately, the paintings are protected. But that house . . .'

'In the name of God, you did well. How terrible it would have been if they'd burned. I'm so upset with myself for not having thought of it,' admits Salah.

'She's right,' interrupts Khaled. 'It would be dangerous for you to show yourselves in the vicinity. So come home with me. I'll alert the Tammar doctors.'

[153]

'No, Khaled, we won't go to your place either. We mustn't put your children in danger. All of you go home, quickly. We're going to return to Tammar.'

'What about your papers?' worries Vincent.

'They're here, in my purse.'

I look at the flames. So many things are burning inside of me. Suddenly, an uncontrollable laugh shakes my chest, paralyzes me, overcomes me, is endless. Salah's arms close around me.

'Calm down, calm down.'

After a moment, through the convulsions of this laughter-sob, I manage to utter, 'Khaled, I'm leaving again tomorrow. Tell the women that even from afar, I am with them.'

In the European Women Writers series

Artemisia
By Anna Banti
Translated by Shirley D'Ardia
Caracciolo

Bitter Healing
German Women Writers, 1700–1830
An Anthology
Edited by Jeannine Blackwell and
Susanne Zantop

The Maravillas District
By Rosa Chacel
Translated by d. a. démers

Memoirs of Leticia Valle
By Rosa Chacel
Translated by Carol Maier

The Book of Promethea
By Hélène Cixous
Translated by Betsy Wing

The Terrible but Unfinished Story of
Norodom Sihanouk, King of Cambodia
By Hélène Cixous
Translated by Juliet Flower
MacCannell, Judith Pike, and Lollie
Groth

The Governor's Daughter
By Paule Constant
Translated by Betsy Wing

Maria Zef
By Paola Drigo
Translated by Blossom Steinberg
Kirschenbaum

Woman to Woman
By Marguerite Duras and Xavière
Gauthier
Translated by Katharine A. Jensen

Hitchhiking
Twelve German Tales
By Gabriele Eckart
Translated by Wayne Kvam

The Tongue Snatchers
By Claudine Herrmann
Translated by Nancy Kline

The Panther Woman
Five Tales from the Cassette Recorder
By Sarah Kirsch
Translated by Marion Faber

Concert
By Else Lasker-Schüler
Translated by Jean M. Snook

Slander
By Linda Lê
Translated by Esther Allen

Daughters of Eve
Women's Writing from the German
Democratic Republic
Translated and edited by Nancy
Lukens and Dorothy Rosenberg

Celebration in the Northwest
By Ana María Matute
Translated by Phoebe Ann Porter

On Our Own Behalf
Women's Tales from Catalonia
Edited by Kathleen McNerney

[155]